AF090909

TASTE OF REVENGE

BOOK THREE
IN THE VAN WILDEN CHRONICLES

Jessica Gleave

Taste of Revenge
The Van Wilden Chronicles Book Three

Jessica Gleave

This book is a work of fiction. Any references to real events, real people, and real places are used fictitiously. Other names, characters, places and incidents are products of the Author's imagination and any resemblance to persons, living or dead, actual events, organisations or places is entirely coincidental.

All rights are reserved. This book is intended for the purchaser of this book ONLY. No part of this book may be reproduced or transmitted in any form or by any means, graphic, electronic, or mechanical, including photocopying, recording, taping, or by any information storage retrieval system, without the express written permission of the Author. All songs, song titles and lyrics contained in this book are the property of the respective songwriters and copyright holders.

ISBN-13: 978-0-6482655-0-4

Editing by Swish Design & Editing
Proofreading by Swish Design & Editing
Book design by Swish Design & Editing
Cover design by Deranged Doctor Design
Cover Image Copyright 2018

First Edition 2018
Second Edition 2019
Copyright © 2019 Jessica Gleave
All Rights Reserved.

DEDICATION

Revenge is sweet but not as sweet as chocolate.
This book is dedicated to chocolate.

GLOSSARY

Primus Vampyrs – Born or alive vampires, originating from the old country.

Primus Vampyr Elders – The oldest of all vampires, the first vampires to walk the earth. Each Primus coven's leader is also their Elder.

First-generation Primus – The first Primus children born from their Elder parents.

Human-turned – Humans who were turned into vampires upon their death.

Daywalkers – Vampires that wish to still live amongst humans.

Night Dwellers – Vampires that only hunted at night and believe they are above humans and only see them as prey.

Dhampir – Half-human and half-vampire. There is only one known Dhampir in existence.

Apotropaic – Substance used to weaken a vampire.

Wolfsbane – Has two uses—to weaken a human-turned vampire, and has the ability to mask a Primus or Dhampir's presence.

Vampire lore – The supernatural laws that governs the race of vampires.

The Council of Order – A group run by the Primus Vampyr Elders to oversee the vampire race.

Agents – Vampires employed by The Council to undertake the tasks of investigating whether a coven has gone bad or not.

Clan – Name given by the Council to vampire covens considered bad.

Coven – Name associated with vampire families.

THE PRIMUS VAMPYRS BLOOD LINES

BATHERAS COVEN
Batheras (nickname Archi, prefers Batheras)
married to Davina (deceased)
Their daughter: Xandria (daughter) married to
Palmer (deceased)
Xandria and Palmer's son: Huntyr

VAN WILDEN COVEN
Octavius aka Oscar married to Delizera (deceased)
Their children:
Jonas
Hector
Mariza

Oscar remarried to Vivienne
Their daughter: Morgana

OLDERMAN COVEN

Gregorius married to Zora (deceased)
Their children:
Titus married to Nari
Their children:
Nardo
Travon

Ezra (deceased) – married to Cabrini (deceased)
Their children:
Dontelle (also Agnor's granddaughter)
Nadine (also Agnor's granddaughter)

Zephyr (has daughter, Clarita with Hammadi's daughter, Laphis)

HAMMADI COVEN

Hammadi married to Jaelyn (deceased)
Their children:
Persiphine married to Endre (deceased)
Laphis (has a child, Clarita with Zephyr)
Walid (deceased)

OLDERMAN/HAMMADI COVEN

Clarita (daughter of Zephyr and Laphis - unmarried)

KALU COVEN

Jelani married to Veynor (deceased)
Their children:
Eshe
Yafeu (deceased)
Ulyara (deceased)

EYDIS COVEN

Agnor married to Matteo (deceased)
Their children:
Endre (deceased) married to Persiphine
Cabrini (deceased) married to Ezra (deceased)
Matthias (deceased)

GETTYBOURGH COVEN

Cleva married to Phoenius (deceased)
Their children:
Palmar (deceased) married to Xandria
Randalf (deceased).

OHANA COVEN

Ohana (deceased) and married to Akineri (deceased)
Their children:
Kaiya married to Hadwyne
Nari married to Titus

WELLCHIDE COVEN
Eleanor married to Leighton (deceased)
Their children:
Hadwyne married to Kaiya
Dorcarthy aka Doc
Patricia

DOVKOSKY COVEN
Ion (deceased) married to Theresa (deceased)
Their children:
Bronten (deceased)
Dieter (deceased)
Vera (deceased)

A NOTE
FOR THE READER

This book has been written using US English but contains some euphemisms and slang words that form part of the UK/Australian spoken word. This series is set in various countries of the world including the UK and Australia.

Please remember that the words are not misspelled, and form part of the every day UK/Australian English lifestyle.

If you would like further explanation, or to discuss the translation or meaning of a particular word, please do not hesitate to contact the author—contact details have been provided, for your convenience, at the end of this book.

TASTE OF REVENGE

BOOK THREE
IN THE VAN WILDEN CHRONICLES

CHAPTER 1

"Again." Svetlana marched across the muddied ground, her boots sinking into the soil. Her blonde hair was pulled into a tight bun at the nape of her neck, making her scowl more pronounced as she watched the line of vampires throwing their stakes in pathetic arcs toward their targets—large hessian bags strung up in the sparse trees lining the edge of their lair. Each were tied with twine about three quarters up the length of the bag to form the shape of a body and head with crudely drawn faces. *They couldn't possibly miss stationary targets.* But this wretched group of scum—from who knows where Ragnorok had recruited them—were throwing stakes like haphazard punches during a two o'clock bar fight and missing the fake Primus dummies by a long shot.

"Keep your arms straight," she barked, turning on her heel and marching back behind them. "You don't vont the Primus filth to get vithin a foot of you. They vill crush your skulls vithout a second thought. Again!"

Their leader and her creator, a tall, lean vampire, Ragnorok, sauntered over to her. He'd changed back into his regular clothes—the white shirt tucked into black trousers and boots. "How are they coming along?"

"You have given me shit to vork vith. No matter how hard I train them, they vill still be shit." Grumblings came from the vampires, but she turned her icy glare toward them, daring each one of them to say another word.

Ragnorok's eyes followed hers. "I'm doing the best I can to replenish our numbers after Morgana *and her motley crew* destroyed that faction."

Svetlana's lips pursed. Yes, she had personally seen to those vampires, turning and trained them exclusively. How they managed to be slaughtered by the leather-clad brat and her two minions, Svetlana didn't know.

Ragnorok gazed at her thoughtfully. "You know if you don't like my selections, you can go out and recruit more yourself. Our plans are moving forward rather rapidly now. I need to remain here more."

Her lips twisted into a smile, and her eyes lit up. "Now *that* I can do."

"Good." Ragnorok straightened. "But I'll go on a last recruiting mission myself." Earning a sharp look from her, he chuckled. "I still haven't found someone to share my bed who satisfies my needs."

Svetlana clasped her hands behind her back, shaking her head at him. "Vee are at var."

"Still doesn't mean I can't enjoy the simple pleasures in life. And I'll need someone to celebrate with after we win this."

Svetlana's top lip curved up as she turned back to the trainees, who had been listening to their conversation. "Did I tell you to stop?" she snapped.

The vampires hastily resumed their stake throwing—still missing the targets—much to her chagrin. "Vee aren't stopping until you hit the targets."

Groans erupted along the line, but she raised an eyebrow at them. Pitiful, the lot of them. She pulled her shoulders back. *But if anyone could train this lot, it was her.*

"Again!"

CHAPTER 2

Oak Wood Hills was a glorious sight during the autumn months. The leaves of the oak trees growing around the small town were changing into golden yellows, bright oranges, and crimson reds.

Morgana took it all in as she walked past the old oak tree in the town center. She couldn't help but zero in on the small carving Gareth had made of their initials in the trunk of the tree. Even from this distance, she could make out the 'GL loves MVW' surrounded by a crude-shaped heart. The tree trunk had been adorned with other lovers' initials, but Morgana only focused on theirs. The sight of it brought a smile to her lips.

Looking around, there weren't too many people about, so she sauntered over to the trunk, the heels of her boots clacking against the concrete path. When she reached the tree, she pressed her hand against the carving, her smile spreading wider. She was so blissfully in love with her mate.

With everything that had happened to her, Gareth, and her family, especially suspecting each other, her ex, Randalf, and Mariza coming to town and letting their issues with Mariza come between them, it had been a lot to deal with. But they were in a good place now in their relationship. They were happy together, something Morgana had been longing for the last two hundred years or so.

Everything in their life was perfect.

Well, except for the mayoral campaign. This was the last week before the election. Their mission cover was coming to an end. And despite the mild scandal involving her siblings being called illegitimate, her father was still ahead of Mayor Coleman. Soon, The Council would grant them permission, and they'd be free to eradicate the Forest Clan. As soon as they wrapped up this case, she was going to take Gareth away somewhere for a well-deserved vacation.

Yes, life was good for them.

She turned away from the trunk. A rush of cold autumn wind blew past her, making her shiver. She tugged at her gray business suit jacket, adjusting the collar of her white blouse to protect her neck from the chill.

Normally, she didn't feel the cold. She glanced around with a strong sense she was being watched.

The Forest Clan wouldn't dare attack her in public like this. Still, she needed to stay aware and always on her guard, especially when she wasn't carrying any weapons on her. The Forest Clan must know their time was coming to an end. Hence, the spying.

But she couldn't quite determine how they were spying on her. Human-turned vampires couldn't use wolfsbane to mask their presence so that it couldn't be one of the Forest Clan. But she could feel eyes on her. Glancing around, there was no one of any interest looking her way, only humans going about their mundane morning routines.

The breeze came again this time, bringing with it falling leaves scattered on the ground around her, a minor distraction. Morgana looked down at the crimson leaves gathering around her black boots. Even though their color was nowhere near as dark, they reminded her of blood.

She shrugged, putting it down to the fact she hadn't drunk any blood for a couple of days now. She turned away from the tree and decided to buy a coffee to stave off the strange chill before she headed back to the campaign office, her boots crunching over the fallen blood leaves.

Tiffini twisted a lock of her chestnut brown hair with her manicured hand. She couldn't wait for the day it would be perfectly preserved when she turned into a vampire. That was one of the cool things about joining the Forest Clan.

But this? Watching these weirdo vampires who had moved into town, she had better things to do with her time than this. Her Instagram wasn't going to post updates itself. She had been selected for the clan because she was rather swift for a human and the tiniest of the recruits, standing at only four feet, nine inches. She also liked to gossip. Hence, why she'd been stuck with this role, but she thought it would have been more fun going back to tell them everything she saw. Except all she was doing was watching a half-breed and the one Ragnorok referred to as a Primus Elder. *Whatever the hell that was.* A few months back when she had first seen the new candidate for mayor and his family, she thought they were human. She'd only ever known about the one type of vampire—dead ones brought back to life. *Man, the books and movies were so wrong.* Apparently, these vampires were *born*. How does that even happen?

She glanced up from checking Facebook on her phone to see the half-breed as the others referred to her, entering the campaign office. The human crinkled her nose. Could her sense of style be any more boring? Just like this spying gig. *So boring.* With nothing more to report there, she stood. Wearing leggings with a t-shirt and joggers, she could pass for a runner… or someone out walking. She began to jog around town looking for the other one.

CHAPTER 3

In the early hours of that same morning, Oscar Van Wilden jogged around the suburban streets. The air had a nice autumn chill to it, providing a good excuse in case he ran into anyone, and they wondered why he wasn't sweating.

Brutus ran alongside him on a leash that was mostly for show. All Oscar had to do was give the dog a stern look, and he heeled. Brutus knew who the alpha male was in their coven.

Oscar found he rather liked Oak Wood Hills when the leaves were changing into a myriad of colors.

He waved to the fellow joggers and other early risers. He had to admit this small-town life was growing on him. If he were human and weren't partially responsible for keeping the vampire race a secret and under control, this would be the type of town he would have liked to live in and put roots down with his wife, Vivienne.

Maybe one day when enough time had passed from this first visit, and they had long been forgotten, he and Vivienne could return and live there for a few decades. That would be nice. His chest expanded at the prospect of moving back to this town.

"Come on, boy." He smiled and gently tugged on the leash. Brutus' tail swished as he followed his master.

Tiffini was tired from jogging around looking for the other vampire and sat on the park bench. She checked her phone to see someone had sent her the latest cat video. Now *that* would be more interesting than watching a vampire run around with his giant dog. A cute dog, nonetheless.

She sat up straighter. *What kind of vampire owned a dog?* These born vampires were so bizarre. Her head tilted at the way the vampire smiled with affection at the dog. Strangest shit she'd ever seen. But then again, the sight of them may be useful to report. Ragnorok was all about using the Van Wilden's familial connections against them. Their greatest weakness.

Taste of Revenge

Tiffini sighed before she stood from the park bench and began walking toward the vampire and his dog.

"What an adorable puppy," she cooed as they drew closer to each other.

The dog's growl made her eyes widen, and she backtracked a bit.

"Don't worry, he won't bite," the vampire tried to reassure her. He looked down at the dog. "We're friendly to the locals." The dog looked up at his master before wagging his tail and approaching Tiffini. She quickly recovered, giving them a fake smile while reaching her hand out to pat the dog between the ears.

"Such a little cutie." She scratched the spot behind the ears that dogs love so much, the puppy preening as she did. "Well, he's not so little. What breed is he?"

"A Tibetan Mastiff." The vampire smiled down at his dog. "He's going to grow up to be about two and a half feet. Won't you, boy?"

"Hey, you're that candidate for mayor, aren't you?"

"Yes, I am. Oscar Van Wilden, nice to meet you." He smiled warmly, holding out his hand.

Tiffini flashed a smile back as she shook it. This vampire really wasn't like the ones she knew or had read about in stories—or the ones her boyfriend hung out with. This one seemed *friendly*. And his hand was warm. *Weird.*

"Well, good luck in the election." Tiffini placed one last pat on the dog's head before running off to avoid the interaction becoming awkward. A little way down the road, she stopped and turned around, pulling her phone out. She pretended to be taking a selfie but had the camera turned around on the vampire and his dog. She took several shots before sending them to her boyfriend. *Too bad she couldn't post those to Instagram.*

It was around eight thirty in the morning when Oscar walked into the campaign office, head held high with a wide grin on his face.

"Phyllis," he greeted his campaign manager, warmly.

"Oscar," Phyllis greeted politely. Usually, she was quite besotted with him, but her attraction to him had soured since his eldest daughter, Mariza, had arrived in town, not to mention his two sons as well. Oscar had more children than Phyllis cared for. Not that he minded the reprieve from her flirtations. The more aroused his campaign manager would get around him, the more difficult he found it to curb his vampire nature.

"How are things going today?"

"I'm very well. Thank you for asking." Phyllis blushed and smoothed her short blonde bob.

Oscar's smiled waned. He hadn't meant to encourage her. His eyes landed on the rush of blood in her cheeks. Phyllis' round face flushed to the same deep, dark, delicious color whenever she was flustered. "I meant about the campaign."

"Oh, yes, sorry."

Again, Oscar's smile faded as her cheeks grew redder. He tried to remain calm and prevent his vampire nature from forcing his fangs to protrude from his gums. *Remember, you must be human.*

"We're still gaining in popularity over Mayor Coleman. We might actually win this."

"Did you ever doubt we would?" Oscar's brow furrowed.

"No, of course not, Oscar. It's just been quite the challenging campaign."

"Ah, but what is life without a little challenge? Otherwise, you wouldn't have come on board, would you, Phyllis?"

"Yes, of course. I'm always up for a good political challenge." Her eyes wandered over Oscar. *Maybe her attraction hadn't soured after all.*

He dearly regretted going all vampire mode on her a few weeks back. She clearly took it the wrong way.

Phyllis smiled, and her cheeks flushed scarlet again.

Oscar's fingers twitched, and he fought the urge to stroke her blood-filled cheek. It had been too long since he'd fed off a live human, ever since the invention of blood bags.

"Have you seen Morgana?" His daughter would certainly put him in his place before he attacked Phyllis during daylight hours and in front of so many human witnesses, who would *not* hesitate to spread the word about their boss being a *vampire*. Humans don't tend to feed off each other, after all.

"No," Phyllis snapped, taking a step back. "They're both late."

Oscar nodded. "I'm sure they'll be along shortly."

"Yes, of course," she said, her lips pressing together tightly.

"Come along, Phyllis, what's on the agenda today?" He held open his office door for her, ever the gentleman. But as she brushed past him, deliberate no doubt, he caught a whiff of her. Not the artificial scent she wore but the smell of her blood simmering under her skin. Her elevated heartrate was making it more pronounced.

He closed his eyes. He was getting worse lately. On the one hand, he needed this campaign to wrap up, so he wouldn't be around humans so much. But on the other hand, he did rather like acting the part of a human. Their mission cover had allowed him to be part of both the vampire and human worlds. So, maybe if he won the mayoral race, he could remain in both worlds.

Ragnorok couldn't believe the *pictures* he saw on the small device Cedric held in his hand. "He has a dog?" he scoffed. "What kind of sick vampire keeps a pet?"

"Well, obviously, that Primus Elder guy," Cedric retorted.

Svetlana snorted. "And are you sure your human girlfriend is correct in vat she saw?"

"These photos were taken minutes ago and sent straight away. Duh."

Ragnorok grimaced when Svetlana shot him a look. As usual, his second-in-command had been right in her opinion. He really shouldn't have recruited the young teenage humans and priming them to be vampires. But this system of using humans to spy on the Van Wildens seemed to be paying off.

"I see." He stood, walking over to the whimpering female human tied up in the corner of the room. He lifted her wrist to his mouth, sobs renting the air as he sank his fangs into her flesh. Smacking his lips, he turned to Svetlana, who was watching him silently. "This is why they shouldn't have their self-imposed control over vampires." He waved his hand in the air. "They're mad, the lot of them." He dropped the human's arm with a thump, tears racking her body. He ignored her and sat back, flicking his hand in the air. "And it's about time I took them down."

CHAPTER 4

That very same morning, Alastor McLoughlin laid back on Ava's bed stretched over the top of the green comforter. He was in the mood just to kick back and do nothing, so he was watching a movie on a portable DVD player with headphones on—some movie about fast cars, unbelievable stunts, and a bunch of surly men and women. Even though the Forest Clan had been quiet for the last few weeks, they'd kept up their patrols at night around town and the perimeter of the forest.

Apart from gathering weapons for these patrols, he'd been avoiding the Van Wilden's home as much as possible. Despite the elation of killing Gareth's creator, his mood was always dampened when he saw Oscar. It felt as if the Primus Elder was trying to impose some sort of guilt, causing Vivienne's brow to furrow and to cast a look between them as if willing them to reconcile. Whatever the case, something didn't feel right, but he let it slide. He had, after all, killed Mariza, Oscar's eldest daughter.

Ava's squeal cut through his thoughts. He lifted the headphones from his ears, letting them hang around his neck as she bounced up and down on the mattress, her eyes shining bright in the glow of the small screen. He had the urge to lean over and flick on the bedside lamp so he could see her hazel eyes in color.

"Guess what?" she squealed.

"What, lass?" He reached out for her, but Ava was still bouncing around on her knees. Alastor dropped his hands, shaking his head at her.

"I have a job interview at the Summerville newspaper. They liked the article I wrote about Oscar and his 'scandalous' children. They want to see a portfolio of my other work. They think I'd be a good fit for their team."

"That's wonderful, love." Alastor beamed. "When's the interview?"

"A couple of days after the election. I'll still be able to cover the story for Dad's paper. I'll have to drive out there, though."

"Do ye want me to go with ye?"

"To the interview?" She stilled, her brow furrowed.

"To drive with ye, of course."

"Nah, it's fine. I can drive myself." She waved her hand at him.

He leaned forward. "But it might not be safe, love."

Ava snorted. "I think it will be far safer there than Oak Wood Hills where it's being overrun with vampires."

Alastor chuckled. "Aye, true, but we don't know how far out Ragnorok is recruiting." His mind raced with the worst-case scenarios for what could happen to Ava on the drive over there.

Ava placed a hand on his arm. "I'll be fine. I'll keep the car doors locked. I'll travel during the day, and I'll go straight from the car to the newspaper building and back out again. Besides, won't they need you here?"

"Aye."

"I won't be gone long." She kissed his mouth before pulling back with a thoughtful look on her face. "What if I bring a stake with me just in case?" She winked. "I mean, how hard can it be to stake a vampire? You just shove it in, don't ya?"

Alastor chuckled. "Nay, love, it takes more finesse than that. But aye, fine."

"Yippee." Ava clapped her hands in delight.

Alastor grasped her biceps, stilling her movements, his voice serious. "But ye call me if ye run into any trouble."

Ava touched his cheek. "Yes, of course. I'll be fine. No one is going to get me out there."

CHAPTER 5

Everything was peachy for Gareth Lloyd.

His evil creator was dead.

He was in love with the most amazing woman.

He had a new role in life as an agent for The Council of Order.

Well, two if he counted the internship at Oscar's campaign office, which was where he was now. The tension was rife in the lead-up to Election Day. Phyllis was even grumpier than usual, stomping around the office, snapping at everyone, except Oscar, of course.

Gareth just shook his head and went straight to his desk to get on with his work. He'd only volunteered here in the first place to find out what Morgana was, and now he was stuck. Part of the cover they told him. Don't ruin it now.

Gah.

Taste of Revenge

He should have just crept after her like a normal stalker. He chuckled to himself. At least he was able to spend time with Morgana at the office. That was the only bright side to being an intern on the campaign. His grin grew wider as he felt her presence drawing near.

"Good morning." Gareth stood and greeted her, planting a kiss on her lips as soon as she entered the office.

"Into PDAs now?" She pretended to look irritated, but he could feel her joy through the bond.

"Only when I can't resist." He winked at her.

Her lips twitched as she tried to remain serious. Their shared bond gave away her true feelings. She leaned forward for another kiss. The sound of Phyllis' heavy footsteps made them step back.

"This is a workplace, not the local night club," she snapped. "Do that on your own time."

Gareth raised an eyebrow. It was only a few weeks ago Phyllis was using their relationship to provide better publicity for the campaign. Amusement filled the bond as Morgana bit back her smile. "Yes, Phyllis."

They both dissolved into silent laughter when the campaign manager walked away.

"I love you." He touched her cheek.

She smiled leaning into his touch. "I know you do." Her returned feelings of love surged through their bond.

Gareth grinned. "You know just because I can feel your love, it's still nice to hear you say it back."

Morgana chuckled. "Fine." She rolled her eyes but offered him a bemused smile. "I love you, too, Gareth."

"See, it's not so hard."

She looked down at his crotch. "No, it's not."

"Bloody hell, woman, we're at the office!" He covered his manhood with his hand. "Can't expect him to jump to attention all the time." Gareth looked around the office, lowering his voice. "But if you're in the mood, why don't we play hooky for the rest of the day?"

Morgana bit her lips, her brown eyes darkening to almost black. "Your place, then?"

"Abso-fucking-lutely." He pressed his now-hardening dick into her hip.

"Gareth! Morgana!" Phyllis barked as she stepped out of her office.

Gareth groaned. "Yep, that killed it."

Morgana covered her mouth, her eyes twinkling with mirth.

"We should have run when we had the chance. She wouldn't have seen us if we'd gotten our vamp on," he muttered.

Morgana shook her head. "It'll all be over soon."

"I can't wait."

"Will you two stop standing around yapping, you've got jobs to do!"

"Sorry." Morgana's voice dropped so only he could hear, "I'll make it up to you tonight." She turned back toward her desk.

He grabbed her by the arm, leaning into her ear and whispered, "Oh, you better, because tonight you're all mine."

After their workday had finished, true to her word, Morgana made it up to him. All night long. She could be quite the dominant one in bed. They'd barely gotten any sleep. Yet he felt more energized than ever before. Drinking blood between their lovemaking sessions had also helped. Now they lay together, their naked bodies wrapped around each other, mint green soft cotton sheets entangled in their limbs.

"What do you want to do after this is all over?" he asked her. Morgana draped herself over his bare chest. His hand absently stroking her back.

"I want to travel," she murmured into his chest.

"Travel?" His hand stilled. "Don't you travel a lot as it is?"

"Yes, but I'm usually stuck in the same place until the mission is over. Then I move on. I want to see more of what the world has to offer, its beauty, and take the time to fully appreciate each place."

"I'd like to do that, too."

"Of course, you're coming with me. Just the two of us. After we finish with the Forest Clan. Take a break from all these missions."

"Sounds good to me." He looked toward the ceiling. "You know I never really thought about traveling to other countries much since becoming a vampire. Thought it wouldn't really be possible."

"You just have to know the right people." She grinned as she lifted her head to look at him. Her face turned serious. "You're not going to be upset if you won't get assigned another mission again so soon?"

"No. I mean, being recruited has been excellent. Truly an exciting time, probably the most purpose I've had in years. But we've constantly been fighting Randalf, Mariza, and the Forest Clan. I mean is that what it's like on all missions?"

"No, this one has been exceptional." She laid back down, resting her chin on her hands looking at him. "So, you won't get bored traipsing all over the world with me?"

He reached up and tucked a strand behind her ear. "Nothing with you could ever be boring. You make life worth living."

Morgana smiled. "I've never been this happy until I met you."

"Really?"

"Truly."

He moved his hand to the back of her neck and leaned up, kissing her. She pushed him back down, deepening their kiss.

Reluctantly, she pulled away, looking toward the sunlight streaming in through the gap between his bedroom curtains and the window. "Come on, we've got to get moving. The election is today. Time to play the dutiful daughter again."

"Have fun with that."

She swatted him playfully. He tried not to wince from her strength. "You have to be there, too. You're an intern."

Gareth placed a hand over his eyes and groaned. "You know I only volunteered to get close to you."

"And look how well it paid off."

Gareth grinned, his cock hardening against her stomach. Her chocolate brown eyes widened, and desire flooded the bond. "Morning sex before we go? We can be quick, you know. There must be a record of how fast a vampire can come."

Morgana tilted her head back, laughing before pressing her lips to his.

"So that's a yes to trying to find out?" he said against her lips.

She groaned, grinding her wetness onto his hardened groin. "Of course, it is."

"Good. Jesus, you're already so wet."

"I'm pretty sure it's leftover from last time, so let's skip the foreplay and get straight to it." She sat up and positioned her thighs around his to straddle him and gently eased down on his shaft.

"I fucking love you," he moaned as he slowly filled her.

She rocked her hips, her head falling back, her dark brown hair that almost looked black in this light cascading down her back. "I love you, too," she puffed. She reached an arm behind her to stroke his balls.

"Jesus, Morgana, you keep doing that, and I'm not going to last."

She gave him a mischievous look. "Well, you said you wanted fast." She sped up her movements, riding him harder.

"And I don't regret saying it either," he groaned, his eyes closing.

Morgana grabbed the headboard to steady herself as she rode him faster, taking it up to vampire speed. Their pleasure climbed higher, nearing the edge.

Morgana ground her hips even faster. He could feel she was close from the way she clenched him. Euphoria flooded their bond. Guttural cries filled the air as they both reached peaks of ecstasy within seconds of each other before crashing down from their shared climax, wrapping themselves around one another.

She laid down on his chest, Gareth still sheathed inside keeping their bodies connected.

"I'm pretty sure we set a record there," Gareth rasped.

Morgana chuckled. Her face buried in his chest.

"If not, we could keep trying."

Morgana laughed and sat up, easing herself off. He felt the loss of being inside her. "We really need to get going. Put our vampire speed into getting ready."

"Celebratory record-breaking sex later, then?" He waggled his eyebrows suggestively.

Morgana smiled, her brown eyes flashing. "Yes."

Gareth propped himself up on an elbow watching her gather the clothes she was wearing to the event. She flashed a playful smile before racing to the bathroom. He sighed and grinned. Lying back on the pillow, he placed his hands behind his head, staring up at the ceiling again.

Yes, life was blissfully perfect.

CHAPTER 6

Morgana and Gareth walked into the Oak Wood Steakhouse, their hands clasped together. The entire restaurant was decorated in red, white, and blue. Dax, the owner, had gone all out for Election Day. He had continued his endorsement of Oscar's campaign even after the news of his older children.

"There you are," Oscar called out to them. Morgana smiled, dressed in her white blouse and pale lavender skirt. The sides of her dark hair were pulled back and fastened at the back of her crown, the ever-dutiful daughter.

Gareth was dressed in dark gray slacks and a pale gray shirt, the sleeves rolled up his muscular forearms. He placed his hands on her hips, pressing his erection into her ass. "I like the innocent-girl look very much," he whispered in her ear.

"Again?" She turned her head to the side to face him, raising an eyebrow.

Gareth grinned. "What can I say? You turn me on."

Morgana bit back her smile. "Well, you better get rid of it."

"Dead puppies, dead puppies." He coughed.

Morgana shook her head, her lips twitching, and her body still thrumming from the aftereffects of their morning-sex session. Hopefully, the election results would be over soon, so they could get back to Gareth's bed.

"You're not helping," Gareth growled, then moved to her side and took her hand.

"Pussy tease," she whispered out of the corner of her mouth.

Oscar waved them over to where he and Vivienne were standing. Amusement flooded the bond as Gareth led her through the crowd toward her parents. They navigated their way through the throng of Oscar's supporters and the other campaign workers, Morgana and Gareth greeting and smiling at everyone along the way until they finally reached her parents.

"Darlings." Vivienne placed her hands on their upper arms, giving each of them air kisses. Morgana refrained from laughing out loud, also feeling Gareth's amusement through the bond. She didn't dare look at him. She wouldn't have been able to stop herself.

"It's an act, Gareth, just put up with it." Her mother sounded like she was chastising him, but her icy-blue eyes were also twinkling with mirth.

Oscar hugged her at that moment. "Nearly over." Morgana pulled back to see he meant more than the mission cover. She nodded, stepping back.

"Gareth, thank you for coming out here today, and for all your hard work on the campaign." Oscar shook his hand.

Gareth was having a difficult time keeping his face straight. She knew he was itching to make some smart-ass comment, but he was trying to behave himself.

"Hullo," Alastor's voice greeted them from behind. Morgana turned to see both him and Ava standing there. The reporter bounced on the balls of her feet, her hazel eyes flashing as she looked around the room. Investigative journalism was Ava's passion, but she could never resist covering any story. Morgana smiled at them.

"Nay, it ain't what you think," said Alastor, interpreting the expression on her face. "She heard The Council might be making their decision any day soon."

"Yes," Ava hissed, her grin wide. "I want to know how it all goes down."

A vibrating noise was heard from Oscar's pocket. He pulled out his phone, frowning at the caller ID on his phone.

"Looks like you'll be finding out sooner rather than later, Ava." His eyes flickered to Morgana, Vivienne, Gareth, and Alastor. "Council," he mouthed to them.

Ava squealed with delight, clapping her hands, drawing the crowd's attention.

"Aye, just excited for the results folks," Alastor told them all.

"Excuse me while I take this."

"But Oscar, they will be announcing the results in five minutes," Phyllis protested, waddling up to them. She'd chosen to wear a lime green business suit today, giving her that frog-like appearance.

"I won't be long." He flashed her a reassuring smile.

"So that's *the call*?" Gareth said, keeping his voice low.

"Yep, the one we've been waiting for," Morgana replied through clenched teeth, plastering a fake smile on her face.

Oscar walked a few steps away, so he was out of earshot of the crowd. The others would still be able to hear, but he didn't want any human ears to perk up.

"Fellow Elders, how say you?" he greeted.

"Octavius." Batheras' deep voice boomed through the cell phone speaker. Usually, Oscar would wince, but Brutus' barking must have desensitized his ears. "It's time."

"Put down the receiver, Batheras, so we can all hear him."

Oscar barely caught the irritated voice of Agnor, one of the female Elders.

The other Elders must be talking through the loudspeaker, their voices distant sounding. Oscar couldn't help but grin. How far technology had come. Gone were the days of using runners as their messengers.

"And what decision have you all made?" Oscar asked before Batheras could retaliate. Otherwise, he and Agnor would bicker for hours.

"Well, as you're also on The Council, we'll need your input as well." He recognized the soft female voice belonging to Elder Wellchide.

"I believe you all know my stance on the subject. As we have recently re-discovered, Ragnorok has a personal vendetta against my family. I vote he die before he attempts to kill one of our own."

Murmurs of agreement sounded where he pictured them gathered in the Elders' chamber room at Headquarters. Ever since the war and the loss of many Primus, including an entire family coven—the Dovkoskys—the Primus had become very protective of each of them. They may not live in the village all together in the old country anymore, but that sense of close-knit community cohesiveness remained—no matter where on the planet a Primus Vampyr may be. Four hundred years ago, when he married a human, the other Primus had accepted Vivienne and Morgana into their fold with open arms.

"Then I think we all know the decision," Gregorus stated.

"So, we're all in agreement?" Batheras asked.

"Yes," came the collective voices.

"Very well. Octavius, you and your fellow agents are to eradicate the Forest Clan."

Oscar didn't realize his whole body had tensed waiting to hear the decision. His shoulders relaxed as he looked toward the others. Both Gareth and Alastor's faces split into wicked grins, Morgana smirked like she already knew the decision, and Vivienne looked pleased.

"Oscar," Phyllis snapped, appearing in front of him. It was extremely difficult to startle a vampire, but somehow, the campaign manager had managed to do so. "Please, end your phone call. They are just about to announce the results."

A female chuckle was heard on the other end. "Well, it looks like we have to let you go get back to being human, Oscar," Jelani chortled.

"Let us know the outcome, my friend," Hammadi spoke.

"Yes, I will. Goodbye."

The Elders bid him farewell, and he slipped the phone back into his pocket. He looked at Phyllis. "Let's go find out who wins." Hope filled his chest. If he won and they rid the town of the Forest Clan, surely, he could stay here.

Phyllis nodded, turning her attention toward the large flat-screen television attached to the bar wall.

The female anchor, dressed in a cobalt-blue business suit, opened her mouth to reveal his fate.

"Well, the results are in, and it looks like Mayor Coleman has stolen victory of the mayoral race from Oscar Van Wilden. This will be Coleman's fifth term as mayor."

The room became a vacuum of sound. Oscar could still hear the soft mumbles of astonishment and commiserations from everyone around him, but he was lost in his thoughts. His chest tightened and neck bent forward. He didn't know why it affected him. It was only a cover after all. But he had put in the effort, and he would have liked the excuse to stay. A hand on his arm brought him back.

"Are you all right, dear?" his wife's soft voice asked him.

"Yes, dear, I'm fine." He tried to give her a reassuring smile and patted her hand, even though they both knew what he was really feeling.

Vivienne gave him *the look*, the one when she knew he was lying. But she nodded her head in understanding. She knew more than anyone how he truly felt about the campaign.

"Well, I can't believe this." Phyllis was affronted.

"You should probably say something to everyone, dear," Vivienne said to him.

"Of course." He patted her hand again and stepped away, clearing his throat. "Excuse me, everyone." The room fell silent. "I'd like to thank you all for your support and efforts during the campaign. We fought hard, but it seems the other man won. Still, that doesn't mean we won't keep fighting for the *right* outcome on the most important issues. Our voices will not be silenced." He turned away. He didn't know what else to say.

The crowd clapped half-heartedly.

"This is all your fault," Phyllis spat at Morgana before lifting her chin in the air and stomping out of the restaurant as best she could through the crowd that was now dispersing.

Vivienne growled, "If anyone is to blame, it's *that* woman."

Morgana stepped forward snarling. "I have never wanted to kill a human so much before."

Gareth had a tight grip on her upper arms, holding her back. "Just think of it this way," he murmured, loud enough for all the vampires to hear, "Now you guys have a good excuse to be out of the public eye for a few days. Seemingly devastated by the campaign loss, you'll be able to concentrate on eradicating the Forest Clan."

"He's right," Oscar agreed. "Why don't you spend the night at the boys' house? Have one last night of freedom, and we'll all re-group tomorrow and strategize how we're going to march on the Forest Clan."

Morgana's eyebrows arched while he was talking, but she nodded in agreement.

"Sorry about the loss, Mr. V." Ava gave him a sad smile before turning away with the others. He caught snatches of their conversation.

"I'm hungry," Alastor mumbled.

"Yeah, we should raid the blood supply."

"I could do with some takeout," Ava commented.

"I don't want human food," Gareth complained.

Morgana moaned. "How 'bout Ava and I get takeout, and you boys can be gluttons on the blood?"

Oscar watched as they walked away.

"Are you sure you're all right, dear?" Vivienne asked, placing a hand on his arm.

He turned to her with a grim smile and patted her hand. "I'll be fine. I think I just need to go home."

Oscar walked into the house and slumped into his favorite armchair.

Taste of Revenge

An excited bark and flash of black fur stirred him from his depressive state. Brutus wagged his massive tail, and Oscar swore his little friend was smiling at him.

The dog must have sensed his somber mood because he placed his head on Oscar's thigh, looking up at him with sad eyes.

Oscar chuckled and scratched behind his ears. Brutus' tail thumped the floor. "You never fail to cheer me up."

The tail thumping grew louder.

"If I didn't know better, I'd say you love him more than me," Vivienne teased. Brutus turned his head to receive a pat from her, then turned back to Oscar.

"A bond between a man and his dog is undeniable. There's something about him that's soothing to the soul. I don't know why I didn't have a dog years ago."

"I know what you mean." She smiled down at Brutus. His tail thumped even louder as he flopped at her feet and rolled over, exposing his belly. Vivienne smiled, bending down to scratch his belly.

"I should make a tasty treat for dinner," she cooed.

Oscar's stomach rumbled. "Yes, I could do with some blood."

Vivienne turned to Oscar, smirking. "I was talking to Brutus. Dax is going to let me bring home some scraps from the restaurant for him."

Brutus righted himself and walked out of the room toward the kitchen. Vivienne winked and trailed after him.

Brutus may recognize Oscar as the alpha, but he knew the omega, Vivienne, was the one who fed him.

Oscar chuckled.

"Don't worry, I'll get your meal, too," Vivienne called out.

And just like that, his mood was lifted.

CHAPTER 7

Back at their house, Gareth reclined on the sofa. Morgana sat on the floor, her legs tucked up underneath her, leaning against his legs.

He looked around the room at his friends, smiling. They hadn't hung out like this since the dinner at Ava's when they tried to suss out whether Morgana was a vampire or not.

The girls were sharing a bottle of wine and giggling about something. Gareth tuned out after he heard the mention of makeup.

Morgana hardly wore makeup. He believed she didn't need it. She was as beautiful today as she was the day he saw her up on that stage in her college-girl outfit. Now he knew better. She was not so innocent, in more ways than one. He adjusted his crotch, his dick getting hard thinking about the ways Morgana wasn't so virtuous.

God, he hoped their little giggle session ended soon. He needed to feel Morgana wrapped around his cock.

She leaned against his legs and nuzzled her cheek into his thigh. There was a spike of arousal from her end of the bond.

"Right." Gareth stretched his arms out, feigning a yawn. "We should get to bed considering we've got a big day tomorrow, killing vampires and whatnot."

Ava covered her mouth but still burst into a fit of giggles.

"Aye, love, we should also head to bed." Alastor winked at his girlfriend.

Morgana stood quickly, her voice serious. "Yes, you should both get the fuck out of the way now. Who knows when we'll be able to do it again." She winked at Gareth, then walked out of the room, ignoring their astonished faces.

Gareth stood. "Well, you heard the lady."

Ava's face turned a delicious shade of red before averting her gaze.

He looked down to see his boner tenting his pants.

"For feck's sake," Alastor grumbled, placing his hand over Ava's averted eyes.

Gareth shrugged. "It's the bond. I feel whatever she feels. It just happens to be manifesting physically."

"Aye, right. The bond." Alastor rolled his eyes.

Taste of Revenge

"Well, hang on now." Ava tried to move Alastor's hand, but it wouldn't budge. "How do we know he isn't telling the truth. I'd like to know more about their bond."

"Love, I'm a lad, and I know what he's thinking." Gareth chuckled. "You heard the boss."

"Aye, go on, ye bastard, git." Alastor swiped his free arm at him.

Gareth ducked and took off after Morgana at vampire speed.

She was crossing the threshold of his bedroom when he reached her.

"Took you long enough," she said, turning her head to the side, her eyes half-lidded.

He grasped her by the waist and twisted her around, fisting her hair. "Don't tease me, woman." He backed her toward the bed, her legs hitting the wooden footboard. Morgana turned them around with her vampire speed, pushing him back onto the mattress. His pants were off in seconds. "Who said I was teasing?"

She reached behind her. He heard the sound of her zipper as she let her skirt drop to the floor before stepping out of the puddled material. She prowled over to him in only her blouse and lace panties. The scent of her arousal consumed him.

He pulled off his shirt, laying back down, his penis at full mast. "Well, have at it, then." He waved at his dick, grinning impishly.

Morgana clicked her tongue, shaking her head, but the bond betrayed her true feelings of amusement. "Gareth Lloyd, if I weren't so horny, I'd reprimand you for speaking to your superior that way."

He raised an eyebrow feigning innocence. "What, you don't like the alpha male?"

Morgana smiled, her eyes full of lust. "You know I like to be in control." She bent down and licked the tip of his penis. A groan escaped his mouth, and his eyes closed in ecstasy. She took him further into her mouth, and his head fell back onto the mattress. "Fuck, yeah."

Her mouth slowly worked her way down his shaft until he hit the back of her throat, and then she slid back up again slowly. She kept repeating the action over and over.

Gareth lifted his upper torso, resting on his elbows. "I thought you weren't teasing me?"

Morgana laughed around his cock before increasing her speed.

Now that was more like it.

The tingling in his balls indicated the pending release just before he spurted in her mouth.

She swallowed every drop.

"Satisfied?" She stepped back, but he knew she was teasing again.

"Not even close." He leaped up from the bed and walked behind her. Placing a hand on her back, he bent her over the edge of the footboard, so her cheek was pressed into the mattress. He peeled off her panties, pulling them down her legs, not bothering to remove them completely before he sheathed himself inside her delicious wetness.

Morgana turned her face into the mattress to muffle her screams as he pounded into her. He raised a hand and slapped it across her rounded ass cheek, making her clench tighter around him.

Even though they did have somewhere to be in the morning, Gareth took his time with Morgana, thrusting into her until she collapsed from multiple orgasms.

He finally shuddered into her and collapsed on top of her before lying on his side and pulling her into his chest as he did so.

After a moment to let her catch her breath, Gareth's toe nudged a hole in the mattress. He let her go and sat up to inspect it.

There was a perfect bite mark in the sheets and mattress cushion.

"You bit my mattress?"

"You kept spanking me while taking me from behind. What was I supposed to do?"

Gareth laughed into the back of her shoulder before pulling back and turning her to face him. "God, I love you."

She grinned, still wearing her blouse. "I love you, too." She sat up, reaching down toward her ankles.

"What are you doing?"

"Pulling my panties back up."

"Nah, leave them off. We ain't finished yet."

Alastor rolled his eyes at the grunts drifting down through the ceiling. "Ye ready for bed, love?" He stroked Ava's blonde hair absentmindedly.

"Yes." Her green eyes were hooded and dark. She looked like she could devour him.

"Don't tell me Gareth's cock display did something to ye?"

Ava giggled, shaking her head. "No, what Morgana said about getting it done before you guys head out on this mission tomorrow did."

"What, ye don't think I'll have the time? For, ye, I'd make the time."

"I don't know. I feel like we should make love before it starts. It feels like it's the right thing to do."

"Aye, yer right." He pulled her onto his lap. "I also want to show *them*," his eyes flicked up to the ceiling again, "how loud I can make ye scream."

Ava giggled into his chest before standing up and pulling him with her. "Well, come on, then."

CHAPTER 8

The next afternoon, Oscar sat in his armchair watching his daughter enter the foyer. Brutus barked and ran over to her, sliding over the hardwood floors, nearly tripping over his large paws.

"Brutus," she exclaimed, squatting down to pat the Tibetan mastiff puppy. Oscar raised an eyebrow when Morgana let the puppy lick her face. Gareth walked in behind her, beaming. He bent down to scratch behind Brutus' ears, who scrambled off Morgana and began pawing at Gareth. Morgana chuckled and patted Brutus along his back, the dog's tail wagging like a pendulum.

Oscar tilted his head. He had never seen his daughter so happy before. The way she gazed at Gareth was the same look the Daywalker returned. He had been right in talking her into coming on this mission. It worked out well for her. Warmth radiated through him, seeing his youngest daughter so happy. He smiled to himself.

Well, at least some good was coming out of the past few weeks of loss and heartache. He stared down at his empty hands. Usually, he held a glass of liquor, trying to be human. Brutus turned and lumbered his way over to him, staring up at him with those big brown eyes. Clever dog. It was like he could sense whenever Oscar was sad and went to cheer him up. Oscar smiled at Brutus, running his fingers through his thick tan and black fur.

"Hello, Father," Morgana greeted. Even her demeanor was friendlier of late. He should thank Gareth somehow for inspiring that to pour out of her.

"Mr. V." Gareth nodded, taking a seat beside Morgana but not too close. Oscar liked that he was still respectful around him regarding his daughter.

Brutus barked, making them all wince—the vampire hearing amplified the dog's decibels. *Maybe that's why vampires shouldn't keep dogs.* But Brutus was part of the family now, and they were never going to get rid of him.

"Brutus, quiet," Oscar commanded. He just needed to train him not to bark as much.

Brutus whined but still scrambled over to the foyer, watching the door.

Alastor entered and stilled when he saw Oscar, who shifted slightly as he gazed back at the

Taste of Revenge

Daywalker. Oscar wished he could alleviate this awkwardness between them, but that would mean telling him, all of them, Mariza was still alive. Luckily for them, Brutus whined at that moment. While the other vampires covered their ears, Alastor's body relaxed, and he chuckled as he scooped up the large puppy with ease. "Aye, ye little brute. I missed ye, too."

Brutus was like a squirming mess of fur.

"He really does like you," Ava commented, a wide grin on her face as she scratched Brutus' ears as best as she could.

Alastor held Brutus out, his feet dangling in the air. "Aye, yer me little buddy, ain't ye?"

Brutus yapped in response.

"Brutus," Vivienne said sternly upon entering the foyer. "Enough with the barking. How many times does Mommy have to explain we have sensitive ears?"

Brutus twisted to look at her, and Vivienne took him into her arms. Once again, Oscar was amazed she let the puppy lick her face.

Oscar smiled, his chest swelling. Brutus was indeed part of their family, and everyone accepted him.

"So, what's the plan here, boss?" Gareth's voice brought Oscar back to the matter at hand. Gareth waved his hand over the maps spread on the coffee table.

Alastor, Ava, and Vivienne entered the living room. Vivienne placed Brutus down onto the floor. The puppy ran straight to Oscar and flopped at his feet.

"Right," Oscar began. "Now that we know the lair is in the old outskirts of town, we should play it safe." Morgana opened her mouth, but Oscar held up a hand to silence her. "Let me finish. If all of us go in with 'weapons blazing,' we'd be playing right into Ragnorok's plans. So, what I suggest we do is go out on patrol, and if you see a Forest Clan vampire, kill it on sight. It doesn't matter what they are doing… feeding, running errands, etc., it's dead. We pick off Ragnorok's army slowly letting his numbers dwindle.

"Another reason we have to play it safe is the new housing developments start in the next week or two, so by keeping the ash piles to a minimum, we won't raise suspicions as to why there are so many piles of ash but no fires."

"Makes sense to me." Gareth sat back, resting his arm on the sofa behind Morgana's head.

Alastor nodded in agreement.

"What about you, daughter? What do you think?" Oscar asked.

Morgana shrugged. "I'm working in a team now, remember? But what I will say is there's been a movement of Forest Clan vampires back in the forest." She pointed at the map—the one the betrayer, Randalf, had left behind. "I think we should also go back into the woods and trail after anyone we see in there. Find out what they are up to."

"Good idea." Oscar rubbed his chin. "But kill them before they lead you into any traps."

"Of course," Morgana scoffed.

"Right, well, that's settled. Keep weapons on you at all times. Keep your blood intake up, and let's start taking these bastards out."

"Oscar, *language,*" Vivienne admonished, but there was a twinkle in her eyes. "Speaking of keeping your blood intake up, are any of you hungry?" She looked at each of them.

"Aye, Mrs. V, I could eat," Alastor said.

"I'll help you, Mother." Morgana stood.

Vivienne's eyes widened at Morgana who merely shrugged. "What? I'm hungry, and I was going to get a snack while I was waiting, anyway."

Gareth smirked at Morgana, his eyes roving over her body, but sobered when he looked toward Oscar. "I'm going to check out the weapons," he said, trying to find a quick escape from Oscar's stern expression.

"Can I come, too?" Ava asked, her eyes lighting up. "I don't think I've ever seen the training room."

"Aye." Alastor offered her his hand when he stood. "Well, then, it's about time we showed ye."

Oscar was left alone in the living room, Brutus now asleep at his feet, his paws twitching like he was dreaming.

Morgana and Vivienne's voices floated in from the kitchen. They kept the volume low, but Primus hearing was second to none.

"You seem happy, dear," said Vivienne as she opened the fridge.

"I'm happy, Mother. Happiest I've felt in a long time."

Oscar smiled at hearing that. He shouldn't be listening and should leave to do something else, but he was curious.

"Well, hopefully, The Council will assign you two together for a mission."

"Yeah, that would be nice. But I don't want to be assigned one straight away."

"I think we all need a break after this one. But I do hope we get more family assignments in the future." Vivienne's voice was wistful.

"I must admit, I was against the idea at first, but I've enjoyed doing a family mission again."

"I'll miss training you and the boys. Maybe I could get Alastor to be assigned with us next."

"You've taken a shining to him, haven't you?"

"Yes, he has such great potential as an agent, even for a human-turned vampire. He will go far."

There was silence before Morgana spoke again. "How's Father?'

Vivienne sighed. "He's tried to hide it, but I know the election results devastated him. I think he thought maybe if he won, we could use that as an excuse to stay," Vivienne's voice was barely above a whisper, "… to continue acting human."

Oscar shifted in his seat, not wanting to hear anymore.

Gareth, Alastor, and Ava were busy chatting amongst themselves as they entered the living room. They fell silent when they took him in.

"Everything okay, Mr. V?" Gareth asked.

Vivienne gasped from the kitchen. "Oh no, your father heard us."

"Yeah, he would. Oh," Morgana gasped, "… the human bit."

Gareth, Alastor, and Ava looked at him gauging his reaction.

Oscar cleared his throat, giving them a grim smile. "Right, then, shall we have something to eat and go kill some vampires?"

CHAPTER 9

They gathered around the dining table. Glasses of blood were placed in front of everyone except Ava, and platters of meat and salads filled the table runner. Brutus was running around the table rubbing his nose into everyone's elbows, and Morgana was sneaking pieces of meat to him every now and then.

Oscar sat back watching them laughing, drinking, and chatting. Here they were, his family coven minus a few members—his other three children. It was a shame they all couldn't get along. It would have been nice to have them all gathered together.

Gareth draped his arm around the back of Morgana's chair. "I don't know how you can eat that slop."

"Don't you like my cooking, Gareth?" Vivienne called out to him at the other end of the table.

Gareth put up his hands. "Not saying anything bad about the way it's cooked, Mrs. V. Just teasing Morgana about liking human food."

"Whatever," Morgana mumbled through her mouthful. "Tastes good."

"I agree," Ava said pointedly, looking right at Gareth. "You've done well, Mrs. V."

"Thank you, Ava."

Laughter ensued.

Oscar cleared his throat, bringing everyone's eyes toward him. "Right, but now that we've all consumed some form of sustenance, we should think about heading out. We'll work in teams. Gareth and Morgana, you'll work as one team, Vivienne and Alastor as another."

"What about you, dear?" Vivienne asked.

"I'm fine to go by myself." He patted her hand. "If I come across anyone, I'm sure I'll be able to handle them. I've been hankering for a good fight since we arrived here. Besides, you and Alastor work well together." Once again, Oscar averted his eyes when he spoke to him. In truth, there was nothing for Oscar to forgive Alastor for. He hated to make the Daywalker feel bad, but he couldn't tell anyone the truth about Mariza.

Brutus barked several times.

Oscar's eyes brightened. He smiled down at the dog, scratching him behind the ears. "No, my little friend, you have to stay here. We need someone tough to guard the house while we're out." Brutus barked again, wagging his tail.

"I swear he can understand you," Gareth said incredulously.

"Of course, he can." Oscar's chest swelled. "We have a special bond, the two of us."

Alastor watched Oscar while he was speaking about Brutus. He had seen the way Oscar cared for his children, and now the Elder had formed the same type of paternal love for Brutus. He only hoped the Elder would make eye contact with him again soon instead of always averting his eyes.

One day he'd earn Oscar's forgiveness for killing his daughter. But for now, he'd just have to deal with the tension between him and Oscar. Besides, they had bigger issues to deal with like getting Ava home safely. He turned away from Oscar and looked to his girlfriend. "Do ye want me to drive ye home, love?"

Ava shook her head. "I'll be fine. I'm too old for them to take me."

"Still a young ruffian to us." Gareth leaned over Morgana to ruffle Ava's blonde hair.

"I'm not that young." She shifted away from him, cringing.

"Still, it would be best to take precautions, Ava," Oscar said. "Let young Alastor take you home. Safety in numbers."

"Wouldn't Alastor be better off staying here to get ready before going out?" she said, standing up. "Besides, I'll just be driving straight home and heading right into my apartment."

Oscar opened his mouth to speak again, but Vivienne placed her hand on his. "Leave it be, dear. Otherwise, you'll be here all night arguing."

"I'll walk ye out to ye car, love, as a compromise." Alastor stood, holding out his hand.

"And we better get a head start, then." Morgana stood, looking at Gareth.

Gareth nodded, gulping down the last of his blood.

"Good luck with the interview, Ava." Morgana held out her arms to Ava. The two girls embraced. "I'm not quite sure when I'll see you again."

Alastor smiled. He loved that the Van Wildens had accepted Ava into the fold with no hesitancy.

"Thanks, Morgana." Ava pulled back and smiled. "Good luck out there, too."

"Luck," Gareth snorted, swaggering past them. "We don't need luck, just pure skill, baby."

Morgana shook her head, but there was a twinkle in her brown eyes.

Alastor stood and sauntered over to his best friend, slapping him on the back of the head.

"Hey!" Gareth turned around to swat him back. Brutus wanted to join in the rabble and jumped up, padding over to them and barked loudly. Alastor was getting used to the dog's bark, but he still couldn't help flinching from the sound.

"Boys, save it for the field," Vivienne chided, though her icy-blue eyes shined in amusement, and the corner of her lips were tugging up.

Morgana clicked her tongue, grasped Gareth's arm, and dragged him toward the basement.

Gareth winked at Alastor before disappearing around the corner and down the hall toward the basement stairs.

"Come on, let's go," Ava said, also grabbing his arm, before sliding her hand down and nestling it against his. He looked down at their joined hands and smiled at the warmth spreading through him from her touch.

"Are ye already for yer interview, lass?" he asked as they walked out of the dining room and toward the front door.

"Yes, as ready as I'll ever be." Her eyes darted around, and she clasped his hand tighter.

"What's wrong, lass?" he asked quietly.

"Can you feel that?" she whispered, leaning in closer.

"Nay, feel what?"

"Like someone is watching us."

Alastor tugged her hand, striding quickly to her car, throwing furtive looks around, but there wasn't anyone to sense besides the vampires inside. "It ain't a vampire, that's for sure. I'd have sensed whoever it was."

Ava clutched her purse closer to her body before sliding into her car and locking the door behind her. He gave her a wave and watched her drive away before turning back to the house. He also couldn't shake the feeling like they were indeed being watched.

CHAPTER 10

Morgana placed stakes into her holster, feeling Gareth's eyes on her.

He stood next to her, his hand hovering over his holster.

"What?" she asked, not even bothering to look at him. She kept at her task.

"There's a weird hyped-up energy coming from you."

Morgana smiled, still placing stakes into her holster.

"You really enjoy this, don't you?"

Her grin grew bigger.

"My little savage." He chuckled and resumed filling his holster.

She looked toward him. "Who are you calling little?" she snarled, though she couldn't mask how her body was reacting, knowing he could both smell and feel her arousal through the bond. Ever since they'd fallen into bed together, they had this strange tug and pull over who had the sexual control—something that thrilled her lady bits to no end. And Gareth knew it.

He looked up at her, smirking before dropping his holster and sauntering over to her. His swagger was slow and deliberate to taunt her.

Gareth wrapped his hands around her waist and brought her up to his height, planting a kiss on her lips. If she'd been standing, it would have left her weak in the knees. He placed her back down, and she stumbled a bit. Okay, it did leave her feeling a little weak. She was totally in love with this stubborn, blue-eyed vampire.

"You ready to get some bad guys, Morgana?" He winked at her. He knew the effect he was having on her.

She steadied herself on his arm—that hardened muscular bicep. She shook her head trying to get her mind clear and focused on the mission. "Target, Gareth. We don't call them bad guys."

Gareth shrugged. "Same difference." He grinned.

Morgana smirked. She stepped toward him, running a finger down his chest. "Unless you've changed your mind about having sex while my parents are in the house, we can do that instead." She looked toward the ceiling where they could hear her parents and Brutus moving around.

Gareth narrowed his eyes and grabbed his holster. "Well played, woman, well played," he growled. "Fine, let's go."

Morgana chuckled as she followed him up the stairs.

Morgana and Gareth didn't have to wait long for a Forest Clan vampire to emerge. They had hidden in the rooftop shadows of the buildings in the deserted real estate development waiting for one of the Forest vampires to get hungry and slip away from the rest to hunt down a human. Ragnorok may have created an army, but they were a greedy army and took more humans than they should.

Their mark was skulking his way over to the back alley near the Old Oak Steakhouse, possibly waiting for a drunk human to come around, stumbling their way home.

Morgana and Gareth grinned at each other before turning back to watch the vampire. No words needed. They both knew what the other was thinking. *Showtime*.

They leaped from building to building following the Forest vampire, both keeping a safe distance, so he wouldn't hear or sense them. Morgana had masked her scent with wolfsbane, but her beating heart always gave her presence away.

When he stopped, Morgana dropped down next to the Night Dweller. He looked young like he had been turned in his early twenties. His body wasn't quite filled out yet, and he still looked gangly. He looked around, his movements were twitchy and uncoordinated like he was nervously waiting for something.

"Ragnorok is recruiting them young, isn't he?" Gareth stepped out from behind a dumpster.

Morgana tilted her head. "How old are you?"

"Twenty." He gulped.

Morgana rolled her eyes. "Not your human age. How long have you been a vampire?"

"Two years, ma'am."

"Don't call me ma'am."

"Yes, ma—" he quickly shut his mouth.

"Do I make you nervous?" She toyed with the stake in her hand and glanced back at the Night Dweller.

"Yes."

"Look, I might not kill you…"

His mouth gaped open.

Gareth's head swung quickly her way. "Huh?"

Morgana smiled, still toying with the stake in her hand. "I'm sure Ragnorok has told you all about The Council and their rules?"

Gareth stood back, his hands up. "Oh, I see what you're doing."

Morgana smiled at him and winked. She usually didn't toy with her targets. She was more of a wham-bam stake-in-the-heart kind of girl. But there was something fun about antagonizing the poor sod. The way he squirmed, his back pressed up against the dirty brick wall. *Maybe Gareth was becoming a bad influence on her.* And maybe she should put this gangly young vampire out of his misery. She turned back to him. "Did Ragnorok tell you about The Council?"

"Yes-s-s," he stammered. "They are egotistical pigs who need to be taken down from their self-imposed pedestals and slaughtered just like they butcher us innocents."

"Innocents?" Morgana laughed. "You must be kidding! The Forest Clan going around destroying half the town's population or turning them. You guys aren't acting very *innocently*."

The vampire drew his shoulders back. "We're just feeding. We have a right to feed."

"Of course, you do. I never said you didn't."

"But—"

Morgana held up a hand. "No, my problem is *how* you're feeding." She stepped closer, her eyes darkening and baring her teeth. "Taking humans to feed is a big no-no."

The vampire backed up against the wall. "You can't kill me, you said it yourself. Unless The Council decides."

Morgana feigned astonishment. "*Did I say that*? I guess I did, didn't I?"

She looked at Gareth who nodded in agreement, a twinkle in his eyes. "You did say that, my love."

She turned back to the vampire, her eyes wide and menacing. "But guess what? The Council decided."

The vampire gulped.

Gareth chuckled. "You're scaring him so much that if he could piss himself, he would."

Morgana bit her lip from smiling, that would ruin the intimidating look she was going for. "And guess what they decided?"

The vampire shook his head, looking around wildly.

"Eradicate," she said, plunging the stake into his heart.

CHAPTER 11

After the others had left, Alastor turned to Vivienne with a wide grin on his face. They were *finally* going to be taking down the elusive Forest Clan. "Where to first, Mrs. V?"

Vivienne smiled. "We'll head out toward the edges of town where there's been the most Forest Clan activity."

"Aye, lead the way, boss." He followed her up the basement stairs and even held the front door open for her.

He cast a glance around them as they exited the house. Alastor still couldn't shake the feeling of being watched. And the others were long gone, so it couldn't have been either of them. He shrugged it off as they trekked to the edge of the forest.

As neither of them were able to wear wolfsbane, they shimmied up different tree trunks, concealing themselves amongst the foliage waiting for a Forest

Clan vampire to come along. After what seemed like an eternity, they felt vampires approaching. Voices drifted over to them before they were able to get a visual. Alastor peered through the leaves spotting a group of three entering the forest.

"I don't see why we have to be the ones to do it," grumbled a curvy brunette, her brown eyes deepened into a scowl, emphasizing her long nose.

Another female spoke, who strangely wore large, blue, square-frame glasses—must have been a cover—her chestnut and blonde streaked hair was piled into a messy bun atop her head. "That's just the way the hierarchy works. We, as the lowly vampires, do these menial tasks while the 'big wigs' take care of the most important jobs. But one day we'll be the 'big wigs' running our own clans. Until then, we put up with it."

The buxom brunette grunted.

"Why is that lass wearing glasses?" Alastor muttered low, so only Vivienne would be able to hear.

"Maybe Ragnorok is recruiting what the humans refer to as hipsters?"

"Feckin' strange if ye ask me."

Vivienne's lips twitched. "We live in a new-age world of human-turned-vampires. May as well get with the times."

Alastor bit his lip to stop himself from bursting into laughter.

Their companion, a male who looked like he'd been turned in his thirties, flung out his arms, halting the two women. "Quiet, you two. Can you not feel that? We're not alone."

"Whatever. We can take them." The brunette flicked her long hair back over her shoulder.

The hipster looked around. "Yeah, I mean the Russian hasn't been drilling us for nothing."

Alastor and Vivienne grinned at one another. That was their cue. Vivienne stood and tiptoed along the length of the tree bough before diving off the end, tucking into a somersault, and landing on the ground in front of them, making the two females squeal and clutch the male.

Alastor's mouth gaped open. *Wow.* His landing was more of a clunky thud as he landed in the dirt, kicking up the dried leaves and littering the forest floor.

They must have looked like a formidable sight. The two female vampires screamed before turning and running. The male sighed and turned, chasing after them.

Alastor and Vivienne took off after them.

Alastor was on the heels of the male, his arm outstretched. He caught the collar of the male, jerking him back, his arms flailing. Alastor reached for his stake. *This was going to be an easy kill.*

As Alastor's hand gripped the weapon, the vampire jammed his foot down onto Alastor's making him release the shirt. The vampire twisted around, his fists flying toward Alastor's nose. Alastor turned his body slightly, avoiding the attack and making the vampire stumble forward, his fist hitting the air.

Alastor whipped out the stake. The vampire quickly corrected his footing and turned back toward him, both of his arms jabbing and punching. Alastor blocked all the attacks. Whoever was training them to fight was good. But he'd had better teachers, and it wasn't long before Alastor's uppercut into the vampire's jaw sent him flying backward landing flat on the ground.

The vampire tried to scramble to his feet, but Alastor stood over him, grinding the vampire's head into the loose earth. "Feckin' bastards." He flipped the stake around as he held the vampire down, plunging the wood into his chest.

Alastor looked up, sensing the hipster nearby. He lit the end of the stake and ran in her direction.

She shrieked when he rounded the tree, stepping out in front of her. Her eyes were wide and darting all around her. *What was with all the screaming?*

Alastor didn't much like the idea of fighting a lass, but she was Forest Clan, and the orders were given to eradicate them. He withdrew a stake, wanting to be done with it. Only hipster vampire had other ideas and ran off again.

"Jaysus Christ," he muttered, giving chase again.

He followed her path, running in an arc, rounding the tree to cut in front of her again, making her jump. Alastor cocked his head. She was newly-turned perhaps and not used to the speed of older vampires?

Once again, she changed direction, scampering off.

Alastor sighed, following her.

When he reached her again, tired of her silly games, Alastor swung his arm out to stop her as she ran past. He had aimed too high, catching her in the face instead, shattering the blue frames, grinding glass into her skin and eyes. Her cries rang through the air. Even he grimaced at the sight of the embedded plastic and glass in her eyes. He took pity on her as she screamed in agony, clawing at her face, trying to remove the shards. He pulled a stake out, lighting the end before plunging it into her chest. Her body spasmed then slumped forward. He stepped back as her body was engulfed in flames.

He turned to see Vivienne had caught the last one, the buxom brunette by her long hair and was dragging her back. She pulled the vampire upright. The vampire hissed in pain as she twisted her neck around. Her eyes were wide as Vivienne smiled at her then sank her stake through the vampire's back ribs.

Alastor grinned. *Feckin' hell. Mrs. V was a badass.*

CHAPTER 12

Svetlana's search had been fruitless. There was no one in this wretched town who was even close to being recruitable. And she was in dire need of sustenance. She wasn't in the mood to head back to the town lair to endure Ragnorok's taunts about returning empty-handed. Creeping around the edges of town, Svetlana spotted a young female with dark brown eyes that were almost black, her raven hair cut at her jawline, emphasizing the roundness of her face. She was rather plain looking, but she'd do.

Before the woman could make a sound, Svetlana plucked her right off the street, her hand clamped firmly around the woman's mouth, stifling her cries. She dragged her back to the edges of the forest away from any prying human eyes.

With her hand still clamped over the meal's mouth, Svetlana pressed her fangs into the exposed neck and pulled them back out, suckling at the essence seeping from the human.

Svetlana groaned, savoring the taste of the fresh blood. Ragnorok would probably want her to turn this one and bring her back as a recruit. But as she drained the body, the girl's skin took on an ashen gray shade that stirred her core. The woman was dying, and that spurned her arousal even more. While technically she was awakened dead, nothing ignited her wanton desire like a dead body.

And eventually, when rigor mortis set in, much pleasure could be attained from stiff fingers.

Svetlana preferred females, but if she were ever lucky enough to come across a male who had died mid-coitus, well, that was a ride she thoroughly enjoyed.

As the female lay limp in her arms, her gaze fell upon the firm, plump breasts she should have sunk her teeth into. *Maybe she still would.* There was something alluring to her about the flavor of dead flesh.

Grasping the neckline of the girl's cotton tee, Svetlana ripped the cloth from the body, exposing the naked flesh. Her tongue swirled around one nipple, but she was interrupted by the sound of a throat clearing behind her.

"It seems I have fallen victim to being a voyeur once again."

Taste of Revenge

Svetlana stiffened. She knew that voice. Raw hatred burned through her veins as she lifted her head to glare at the vampire standing tall and proud before her. His brown eyes stared into hers with mutual disdain. Oh, how she hated Oscar Van Wilden.

The entire reason she put up with the ramshackle of an army Ragnorok had assembled was so she could enact her revenge against Oscar for killing her brother. Gregovich had only been a vampire a short while before he'd been killed. Svetlana had still cared for him, even though he'd slaughtered hundreds as he fed.

"It's the blood lust, sister. I can't control it." He would plead to her when he returned every morning, and she'd forgiven him.

She understood now the hunger a vampire experiences. Night Dwellers were meant to rule this world—be free to do what they must. Feed and kill, not hide away from the humans. The humans were their food, their source of life.

Ragnorok's cause was just. Once they had killed The Council and freed their kind from the shackles of this self-imposed organization, they would be free to do as they willed.

Gregovich couldn't help his new nature. That's how vampires are. But Oscar had killed him for the humans' deaths, for bringing attention upon himself, citing reasons unfathomable to her.

Ragnorok had also been there that night. He'd told her he was too late to save her brother. But he spoke of promises to help her get her vengeance if she let him turn her.

Oscar's hands moving to the belt of stakes strapped around his waist brought Svetlana back to the present. She snarled, dropping the human to the ground and stood slowly.

If she were to fight the Primus, she was not going to be in a comprising position. She bared her teeth. Her only regret was they had not discovered the secret of killing the Primus from Oscar's whoring spawn.

She lunged at the Primus, aiming to wrench one of the stakes from around his waist and stake him with it, giving her ample time to flee.

But the Primus was quick to block her attempt. Her hand whipped forward but was blocked again. She twisted to the side, trying to get at him from another angle, but he anticipated her moves, grabbing her wrists.

Svetlana grunted, tugging her arms to free herself from his grasp. She hated to admit the Primus was a skilled fighter—something she hadn't considered when making her vengeance plans. But plans can always change. She just needed to be more cunning about her attacks.

Their arms flew back and forth as they attempted to block each other from reaching the stakes.

Svetlana grinned as her hand enclosed around the length of one of the wooden weapons. She flashed him a cocky grin before her hand shot out toward his chest.

The Primus grunted and looked down at the stake she'd plunged into his chest.

She smirked at finally achieving what she'd strived for all these years.

"That isn't going to kill me." He grasped the end of the stake and pulled it from his body.

She lifted her chin. "Vell, I still enjoyed doing it."

Stepping forward, the Primus smiled at her. "I'm sure you did." He flipped the stake around before a piercing pain spread from the front of her chest. Her body fell backward. The Primus caught her before she hit the ground. "But that's how you kill a human-turned vampire."

Svetlana's eyes widened as the stake slid further through bone and sinew before touching her heart. Her eyes looked up toward the sky before descending into darkness.

At least now she would be reunited with her brother.

Ragnorok hated this room. He cast his eyes around the scruffy red velvet furniture. Whoever had owned this house had horrible taste, especially for a human. His first thought had been the furniture might hide the bloodstains that were likely to occur, but they'd only dried in large patches into a vulgar brown color. He didn't really like to use this room. This was where Mariza had sat and listened to their plans, all the while planning on betraying them. But Svetlana insisted he needed a chamber room to address his clan members.

He looked up to see Nasir standing there waiting to report whatever drivel he had to say. Ragnorok waved his hand allowing him to speak.

Nasir bowed his head. *Always so formal.* "They've begun their assault on us, my Lord."

Now *that* had his attention. He lifted his head sharply. This was much earlier than he had anticipated. It had taken them longer to make a move on the Obscure Clan.

"How many have we lost?" Ragnorok asked.

"Five and counting, my Lord."

"Who have we lost?"

"The Irish and the blonde took out the trio heading into the woods. The halfling and her mate took out Wes in town."

"What game are they playing taking us out one by one? That isn't usually their style." Ragnorok scrubbed his face before looking at the vampire again. "Why did Wes leave the compound?"

Nasir's head dipped down. "Forgive me, my Lord, but the men are finding it boring to stay indoors all the time."

"Well, tell them to fucking get used to it. They're fucking Night Dwellers now!" He stood. "Where's Svetlana?" She would knock some sense into them.

"Still on a recruiting mission."

"Great, just fucking, great. Let me know the moment she returns!"

"Yes, my Lord."

Ragnorok cursed under his breath. "And bring me someone to drink!"

CHAPTER 13

Oscar returned home to find Ava sitting in the living room. Brutus' head was in her lap as she stroked his black fur. "My dear, what are you doing here?"

"Sorry, I couldn't help myself. I came back here waiting to see how it all went down." Ava turned to look at him. "You know, for a bunch of paranoid vampires, you tend to leave the door unlocked a lot."

Oscar smiled, walking toward his armchair. He looked at Brutus, who barely lifted his head, continuing to preen under Ava's touch. "Yes, I suppose we rely on the uninvited barrier a little too much. But we never think about humans entering the premises."

"Maybe you should."

He felt the presence of the others returning to the house. Brutus jumped up and ran to the front door, barking madly. They all trudged inside.

"How many?" Oscar asked, standing to pour himself a whiskey.

"We got one," Gareth replied.

"Aye, I staked two, and Mrs. V got one."

"Dang, I'm gonna have to up my game."

"Ye should have seen Mrs. V fight." Alastor jerked his head in her direction. "She's a tough mother."

"Yeah, I've seen her take on Mariza—" Gareth's voice trailed off, his eyes flickering toward Oscar. His lips thinned. There was an awkward silence before Morgana spoke.

"Well, it's not a competition, boys." Morgana placed her hands on her hips before smirking. "Because if it were, I'd beat both your asses."

Oscar chuckled.

"Hang on!" Gareth exclaimed. "I thought we were on the same team?"

"We're all on the same team," Oscar said, silencing the room. "But if it's a competition you want," he smiled, "I'm afraid to tell you I have you all beat."

Morgana crossed her arms over her chest. "How?"

Oscar raised his glass at her. "I killed Svetlana, dear daughter."

"No way."

"Way to go, Mr. V." Gareth sounded impressed.

"Very impressive, dear," said Vivienne.

Brutus barked his approval. Oscar smiled down at the dog and scratched him behind the ears. "Yes, it will certainly turn the tide in our favor. We should have the end of this mission wrapped up within a week or so."

"Maybe we should start taking more on now?" Morgana leaned forward.

"We've only cut off the right arm, not the head. Stick to the original strategy for now. We'll amp up our game once their numbers have dwindled significantly. Remember, they are residing in town, and we don't want to draw the humans' attention." He took a sip of whiskey. "The last thing we want is The Council sending in the team trained to deal with that type of situation." *Though he thought it would be nice to see his youngest son, Hector, again.*

"Fine. But I still say that's a boring way to do it." Morgana sat back.

Oscar's lips twitched. "Very well, we'll continue our efforts tomorrow. Drink to regain your strength and rest up."

"Aye, I might sit this one out." Alastor placed an arm around Ava's shoulders. "Ava's got her interview tomorrow in Summerville."

"I can drive myself up if you're needed here," she said to him.

"Nay, lass, it ain't safe for ye."

"He's right, you know," Oscar said. "It's not safe to be out there on your own, especially with the death of Svetlana. Who knows how they will retaliate after they discover her ashes."

Ava opened her mouth but closed it again as Oscar leveled her with his stare. The Primus Vampyr Elder stare even caused Alastor to sit up straighter and Gareth to shy away. That stare had been something he'd been perfecting for years.

"Well, if that's settled, we'll reconvene tomorrow night."

The rest of them nodded and all went their different ways.

"You seem to be in a better mood, dear," said Vivienne.

Oscar patted her arm, giving her a grim smile. "Just taking it all one day at a time."

"I'm exhausted." Morgana sank on the edge of her bed. "That's the worst part about this job. The long night hours."

"I hear ya. Who knew picking off vampires could be so draining?" Gareth sat beside her, bending down to take off his shoes.

Morgana craned her neck, trying to massage the kinks out.

"Here, let me." Gareth's fingers replaced hers. She groaned, her eyes closing at his firm touch. "Your hands feel so good."

Gareth chuckled. "Too bad we're not alone at my place, then I could really show you ways my hands can make you feel good," he murmured into her ear.

Morgana's eyes flew open, and she twisted her torso to face him, giggling. "I still don't understand why you won't touch me when we're here?"

Gareth's hands stilled, embarrassment filling their bond.

Morgana covered her mouth as the giggles erupted. She fell on to the mattress holding her stomach.

Gareth looked away. "Well, it's kind of fucking awkward having them around. I don't exactly want them hearing how I make their daughter scream my name."

Morgana sat up and wiped away the tears that had formed, clearing her throat. "But we're all adults here, Gareth. They know we are mates and will be having sex."

"I know, but one is my boss, and the other one trains me. *Vampire hearing sucks.*"

Morgana grinned.

Gareth leaned over to her smiling. "Stupid, I know."

Morgana chuckled. "Very stupid."

He shrugged. "I still have my nineteenth-century morals and values ingrained in me."

Morgana's eyes twinkled. "You're cute, do you know that? I'm too tired to do that, anyway."

Gareth chuckled. "You know it would be nice if we could live somewhere on our own."

She reached up and touched his face. "Maybe when this mission is over and after we take a break, we'll get assigned together because of our bond, and then we can do that."

"Sounds good to me."

Morgana opened her mouth to continue, but a yawn escaped.

Gareth grinned. "We'll talk more about it later. Right now, let's get some sleep."

Morgana nodded, her head falling onto the pillow.

"My Lord." One of the human spies Ragnorok had sent out came running into the sitting room—Tiffini with three i's. *Humans were becoming deplorable with name choices for their spawn.*

"What is it?" he said with resignation. After Nasir's reports, he needed a *drink*.

"It's Svetlana."

Ragnorok followed the young human and Cedric to the edge of the forest staring at the object before him. Ragnorok stood over the body as it was engulfed in flames and turned to ash, her presence fading into nothing.

His Svetlana.

He never told her he held a special place in his heart for his creationling. So proud of her he was of the vampire she'd become and how she trained his armies. Now her life was no more.

A roar erupted from his mouth.

There was no taint in the air of their presence, but he knew it was *them* who had killed her. Whether it was the half-breed, her betrayer of a mother, or the Primus Elder himself, this death had their mark all over it.

He hissed at the pile of ashes before retreating to the town lair. "Gather everyone," he barked. "We're moving."

"Again?" Cedric asked.

"Yesss," he hissed. "Just do what I say."

It was time to put his modified plans into motion.

CHAPTER 14

Morgana didn't even remember falling asleep. She stirred from her slumber to see sunlight streaming through the window. She opened her eyes when she couldn't feel Gareth next to her. Looking down at herself, she was still wearing her leather pants and shirt. Gareth must have pulled her shoes off for her. Reaching for her phone, Morgana saw it was ten o'clock. He must have let her sleep in, and that brought a smile to her face. Reaching out, she felt his presence at the campaign office.

Her brow furrowed. *That's odd—what was he doing there?*

She turned to his pillow and found a note in his scrawl. Morgana sat up to read it.

> *Morning, sleeping beauty,*
> *You probably can tell where I am. Helping your old man clean out the office.*

Jessica Gleave

Apparently, Phyllis is AWOL.
Love you,
Gareth

Morgana frowned at the note and grabbed her phone. She quickly dialed her father. He answered on the third ring.

"Good morning, dear."

"Morning. Do you think Phyllis has been taken? Is that why she's missing?"

Oscar sighed. "I think Gareth may have exaggerated the situation. No, she's not missing as far as I'm aware. She emailed in her resignation letter with a forwarding address. She moved to another town looking to build her career."

"Oh, good." Morgana placed a hand on her heart.

"If I didn't know any better, I'd say you were worried about my ex-campaign manager?"

Morgana laughed dryly. "No, more worried she'd see us when we finally confronted Ragnorok, and she'd find out we're vampires. The last thing I want to deal with is her screeching."

Oscar chuckled. "Ah, true. What are your plans for today?"

"Well, I thought we could head out to see if we can do some more recon on the town lair, see if we can take them out in one go. It's slow-going picking them off one by one."

"Yes, it has been tedious. I may have been wrong to think that would be the better strategy. Well, Gareth and I'll be detained for a while longer here. Alastor is still with Ava for her job interview in Summerville, and your mother is on a *grocery* run. It seems our supplies are running much lower now that our coven has grown."

Morgana could picture her father looking at Gareth as he said this. Gareth and Alastor were often raiding the Van Wilden's blood supply. She could hear Gareth's incoherent mumbling in the background.

She chuckled. "Do you want me to wait, then?"

Oscar hesitated before answering. Now that the Forest Clan knew of her weakness to silver, it wasn't the ideal situation for Morgana to go out on her own. But they both knew she liked her independence. "No. I think if you're just observing, then you will be fine to go on your own. Just keep far enough away in case they try to use silver on you."

"Fair enough. I'll report back later."

"Good, then we'll all head out tonight to eradicate more of them."

"Sounds like a plan."

"Be safe, my dear."

Morgana snorted. "Always."

CHAPTER 15

Ava couldn't mask the grin on her face the entire time she sat across from the two interviewers—Editor in Chief, Jeffrey Roads, and the newspaper's HR Manager, Anissa Poe. She'd tried to remain as professional as she could, but her heart was thumping like a racehorse gunning for first place even as the interview was drawing toward the end.

"What do you think about the concept that the press is dying?" Jeffrey leaned forward resting his elbows on the conference table. His hazel eyes, more gray than green, reflected in his irises, scrutinizing her. Signs of middle age were prevalent in the editor—short gray hair, sprinkled with flecks of white, framed shallow wrinkles lining his skin. Having recently turned fifty, he'd been the editor of the paper for as long as Ava could remember.

"I don't think the press itself is dying. People still read news stories, they just access them through their phones. Print media production is down, but I don't think it will ever truly go away. People still like the feel of paper in their hands while they read and drink their morning coffee. Besides, how else will people line their pets' cages if we don't supply it to them?"

Jeffrey and Anissa exchanged looks before chuckling. "You've got a sense of humor to you. I like that." Jeffrey pointed his finger at her.

"Well, I think we've got all we need from you to wrap up this interview," Anissa said, raising her perfectly arched dark brown eyebrow. Her burnt amber eyes had been watching Ava closely through the entire interview. "Unless you have any more questions, Ava?"

"No, I think I've asked all my questions already." Ava smiled.

Jeffrey chuckled again. "You certainly do take the initiative to ask questions when needed."

"Thanks, Ava, we'll be in touch." Anissa extended her mocha-skinned hand, giving her a warm smile.

Ava shook her hand, then Jeffrey's, and walked out of the interview room, pleased with the way it had gone.

Anticipation escalated within her as she passed the other writers in their cubicles plucking furiously at their keyboards. One of these spaces could soon be hers.

Outside, leaning against her car, Alastor waited.

"How did it go, love?" He pulled her into his strong arms.

Ava pulled back to gaze into his eyes. "Really well. I think I'll get it."

"Of course, ye will. Never doubted it for a second."

Ava grinned before kissing him.

Small vibrations radiating from his pocket pulled them apart. He frowned and pulled out his phone. His frown deepened when he read the message. "Sorry, lass, to cut the celebrations short, but we need to head back."

"What's wrong?"

"Morgana went off on her own."

Ava's eyes widened. "She knows not to. Why didn't the others stop her?" She hurried as best as she could in her patent pumps around to the passenger side.

"They said she was just making a scouting trip. But ye know the lass, she seems to attract fights."

"Yes, she does."

"I'll need to drop ye off at home before I stop by the Van Wildens."

"Of course." Ava had barely buckled herself in before Alastor was peeling away from the curb.

Taste of Revenge

Ragnorok watched the two lovers embrace outside of the newspaper building. He usually didn't recruit this far away from the lair, but a hunch had told him to go to Summerville.

He was far enough away that his presence wouldn't be felt by the Irish Daywalker. But that was the beauty of exceptional vampire sight. He could still see them as clearly as if standing only a few feet away.

The blonde human was the right age.

And she kept herself healthy, judging from her trim figure, though he much preferred a woman with curves. Angelique had ample bosoms.

The thought of his creator spiked his anger.

How much of a blow and payback would it be to the Daywalker if he took his mate?

When Ragnorok had arrived in Oak Wood Hills, he had been happy to leave the two local vampires who had resided in town long before he arrived, alone—even thought of recruiting them. But they had taken up with his enemy. His original plans had only included vengeance against the Van Wildens, but now they included the Irish Daywalker by association.

Ragnorok smiled and decided to rush back to Oak Wood Hills. He would take her from there in the presence of the Daywalker.

CHAPTER 16

Morgana crouched patiently on top of the building—the same one she and Gareth had scouted from the night before. Something appeared to be wrong, though. Last night there were plenty of vampires around. Now there was no one. *Maybe she was here at the wrong time of the day?* The Forest Clan were *Night Dwellers* after all. But she waited until she saw, or rather felt, a vampire emerging from the forest, creeping toward the town-lair house. He was young, barely an adult, she guessed—short, messy dark hair fell down around his pale-skinned forehead and into his eyes. He flicked his head to the side, clearing his line of sight. Ragnorok was recruiting those *emo* humans now?

But what struck her was the fact he was coming from the forest.

She sat and waited as he entered the town lair, and then re-emerged soon after carrying a young human girl.

What was he doing with her?

Either she was dead or being turned. Morgana strained her ears to hear a heartbeat.

Nothing.

She watched the vampire head back into the forest. Every now and then, brown eyes which bordered on being black flicked in every direction.

Morgana raced through the woods after him. He was quick, but she was faster.

The Forest vampire stopped suddenly, and Morgana had just enough time to jump behind a large tree trunk as he looked around. She peered around the tree trunk and saw him jump fifty feet into the air. Morgana decided this was as good a time as any to blow her position, and she raced over to the spot where the vampire had disappeared. She looked up at the forest canopy above her. Taking a deep breath and preparing the muscles in her legs, she settled into a slight crouching stance then jumped up to the tree canopy to follow the Forest vampire.

Nearing the top of the canopy, she grabbed a branch, swinging herself around to land gracefully as a cat atop the branch. She quickly scanned the scene. The vampire was nowhere in sight. She closed her eyes to concentrate on picking up the vampire's scent. He was some ways ahead, northwest of her position. She turned and leaped from branch to branch following the scent.

Eventually, she caught up with him and saw the vampire stop as he reached a clearing where other vampires were milling around.

"Where does Ragnorok want them?" he asked another young male vampire.

The other vampire motioned with his head. "Over there, back by the others." The vampire sniffed the air. He looked up at the canopy, his eyes locking with hers where she was perched on the tree branch. She gave him a sly smile.

"Shit, she's here." He backed away, the others flanking him.

The vampire she had followed turned his head toward her.

Morgana smiled and dropped down to the ground behind them. "I guess you weren't expecting me."

A cruel laugh sounded behind her, making her skin erupt with goosebumps—that cold, menacing presence so familiar to her now. "On the contrary, my dear, we've been waiting for you."

"Ragnorok." She lifted her chin, staring him down. "Ready to die today?"

Ragnorok smiled. "Not me, you." He snapped his fingers, and vampires began emerging from the trees. They surrounded her like pack animals circling their prey. She counted only ten of them. She almost rolled her eyes. Morgana smiled, stretching out her neck and loosening up her limbs. She was looking forward to a good group slaughter. It had been a while since she fought on her own. Nowadays, she was always fighting alongside Gareth and Alastor. She liked their company, but there was nothing more satisfying than a solo battle and a long moment of triumphant solace while turning them all to ash afterward. And her father had never said she couldn't kill them if they ambushed her.

Each of her hands each wrapped around a stake, pulling them from the leather holster belted around her waist. Without looking, she threw a stake behind her, catching a vampire in the throat. He made a gurgling noise as blood bubbled out of his mouth. She threw the other stake directly into his heart.

She turned back and cocked her chin toward Ragnorok whose mouth gaped open. "No, I don't think I'll be the one dying today," she said.

Snarls and grunts filled the air as the others began to advance on her.

She ducked one vampire, flinging her leg out to kick another. Her heart raced, and a wide grin spread across her face. *Finally, some fun.*

She drew out two more stakes as the vampire to her right lunged at her. She ducked, stabbing the vampire as he flew overhead. The next vampire was on her back within seconds, a third came in from the front. She smiled to herself. She hadn't had a good group fight on her own for a while now. Well, it had to have been at least two or three weeks.

She punched the vampire in front and threw a roundhouse kick to the other. The vampire at her back grasped her around the neck. She flipped the stake backward, goring him in the stomach. He released her, and she turned, withdrew the wooden weapon, and staked him straight through the heart.

"Uh uh uh," another vampire tutted, shaking his finger at her. *Crap, where did he come from?* Also, where did Ragnorok find these recruits of his? Some of them didn't look old enough to be off their mother's boobs let alone turned into vampires.

Morgana huffed and straightened herself, preparing for his attack. The vampire smirked, whipping out a silver knife flashing it at her.

"Shit." She backed away as the rest of them advanced, her eyes drawn to the objects they held in their hands.

"You dirty bastards." *Who brought silver knives to a stake fight?*

Morgana usually relished being a lone agent, but now, with a mate who loved her and a healthier relationship with her parents and new friends, she had more to lose if she were to be weakened by the silver or worse. She gritted her teeth. She did not like running from a fight, but even a skilled and ruthless fighter knew which battles to choose. Continuing this battle was not a winning strategy. She turned on her heel and ran straight for home.

Ragnorok shook his head. "I'd have never picked her for being a coward. Such a pity." He drew the shotgun from the back of his waistline. He glanced around at his followers, all standing around looking at each other, unsure of what to do. "Well, don't just stand there, go after her, you fools. Go on!" He waved his hands in her direction, shaking his head, "Fuck sake," he muttered. Another reason to hate the Van Wildens. If they hadn't killed Svetlana, these idiots would have been whipped into military shape by now. How he missed his second-in-command.

Morgana felt them on her tail. She pumped her legs, trying to run faster than was already possible. Her path was clear—all she had to do was run through the front door, and the barrier that kept uninvited vampires out would protect her. She raced toward the porch steps when she heard the click of a gun's safety. Morgana snorted. They brought *a gun* to a vampire fight.

Her mind flashed to the gun and box of bullets in her own basement. She knew the Van Wildens wouldn't be the only ones to have obtained silver bullets. They were extremely rare, found only in a select few black markets across the globe.

Oh, fuck.

She heard the barrel of the gun turning followed by the loud bang as the gun was fired.

The bullet hit her bicep, an excruciating burning pain spread down her arm. Her vision darkened immediately.

Morgana placed her hand on the wound, trying to stem the blood pouring out. Her breathing became ragged. She needed to move, but her strength was leaving her. Yep, she guessed it. Silver bullets. Man, not a good time to gloat that she'd been right. She staggered forward and fell to her knees.

That all too familiar presence approached her.

She turned to face her shooter. Through blurry eyes, she looked up to see Ragnorok looming over her, smiling at her with a gun in his hand.

She lifted her chin, trying not to show him how much pain she was in.

"Such an amazing weapon, the gun is." Ragnorok turned the shotgun around in his hand. He squatted down in front of her. "And with silver bullets. Such an ingenious idea."

Taste of Revenge

He fired another shot, and the bullet pierced her stomach. The smell of her blood reached her nose. Other vampires were approaching, their eyes glowing, fangs visible.

Another shot fired at her left shoulder. The bullets tore into her flesh. As if being shot with one bullet wasn't painful enough. But three?

Her body felt like it was on fire.

"Silver bullets won't kill me," Morgana rasped.

"But they have made you weaker. Notice I didn't aim for the heart. I only wanted you weakened."

As much as she hated to agree with him, he was right. The silver was like a slow burn consuming all her strength.

The excruciating pain spread from each wound, making her eyes tear up.

There was also anguish and fear mixed in with her pain.

"Gareth," she rasped, her vision becoming unfocused. The last thing she heard was Ragnorok's cruel laughter before it all went dark.

CHAPTER 17

It was a long and grueling day clearing out the campaign office, but Gareth was never happier at the thought of not seeing that place ever again. He and Oscar had returned to the Van Wildens to ready themselves to go out scouting with Morgana.

"Not many left," he noted, pulling stakes out from the wall holders.

Even after he and Morgana had whittled so many stakes for their punishments, the numbers were dwindling.

Oscar grinned. "It's a sign the mission is nearing an end."

Gareth nodded, placing a stake into his leather holster when the peripheral of tan and black fur caught his attention.

Oops. Someone had left the door to the training room open, and Brutus had wandered in. The inquisitive puppy walked around the room and stopped to sniff at the wooden training dummy. Just as he was about to cock his leg, Oscar barked, "Brutus!"

The puppy looked up at Oscar with his big brown eyes.

Gareth bit his lip, trying not to laugh.

Oscar was by the dog within seconds.

"Sorry, Gareth, you're on your own. I need to let this one outside."

"Sure thing, Mr. V."

Oscar nodded, carrying Brutus up the stairs. "You know you shouldn't be down here. Out to the backyard with you, mister."

Gareth smiled and shook his head, continuing to refill the holsters.

He thought of Morgana and felt for where she was. He tilted his head. *Huh.* She seemed to be approaching the house—at quite a fast pace.

Then he sensed the presence of more vampires, and loud bangs rang through the air. His eyes shifted to the shotgun and the box of silver bullets locked away in its case.

"Morgana!" Gareth cried out. His body was overwhelmed with fear and pain. Then the bond severed, and he couldn't feel her. For the longest time, he had only known the bond and her feelings mingling with his. Now it felt like half of him was gone.

Oscar's roar sounded from outside, but Brutus' howl reflected how he truly felt. The Elder was beside him again within seconds, but Gareth ignored him, tearing out of the room and out the front doors.

She was gone.

They all were.

All that remained were splashes of blood on the ground.

He could feel the residue of vampires, and he followed them.

Oscar had taken the little rascal out to the backyard. He leaned against the pole nearest to the back steps watching Brutus sniffing each bush or pawing at the ground. It brought a smile to his face.

It really was a nice place to live. Brutus especially enjoyed himself. Maybe after the mission was over, they could stay here for a bit and relax. He gazed over the back porch. He should install a hammock out here. Morgana would like that.

Brutus' growl caught his attention—the puppy on his back haunches, his fur raised as he looked toward the front of the house.

Oscar felt it. The oncoming presence of a horde of vampires approaching the house. A human mixed in with them. Morgana.

Taste of Revenge

Oscar raced back inside and down to the basement, gathering up as many stakes as he could. There was no time to holster them with the threat of an immediate attack.

Loud bangs rent through the air.

Oscar stilled before a roar erupted from his body. Brutus howled from above.

Gareth flew up the stairs, Oscar at his heels. The scent of his daughter's blood stopped him. The stakes in his arms clattered to the ground.

No. It could not be.

Coldness washed over him, his heart clenching in his chest. Not another daughter.

He touched the patch of grass where her spilled blood had fallen.

He shouldn't have let her go on her own. Not only had he failed her as a father but as her coven leader as well.

A mass of black fur flew past him chasing after Gareth.

"Brutus, no!" Oscar caught him up in his arms, making the puppy yelp. "I'm sorry, but you'd be no help out there with him."

"What the feck happened here?" Alastor said, suddenly appearing.

"Quick go after him. I need to call Vivienne."

"Aye." Alastor took off after his best friend.

Oscar's lips thinned as he carried the squirming puppy inside, looking around for his phone. This was one phone call to his wife he didn't want to make.

The Forest Clan vampires were traveling through the edges of the forest for cover and making their way back to their lair on the outskirts of town.

Gareth charged in not caring if he was armed or not. They had his mate.

He nearly stopped at the realization of what he'd called her. Usually, he just referred to her as his girlfriend, which didn't really matter now. They had her either way.

He flew through the front door, searching the rooms. The lair was empty.

They had led him here to throw him off. *Fucking bastards.* The first clue that should have alerted him was the fact he could enter the mansion.

"Fuck." He lifted a chaise and tore it in half, throwing the pieces against the wall.

He hadn't prepared and ran straight in blindly chasing after her.

"Where is she?" he cried.

He knew someone had followed him. He had been paying attention to who it was, but his best friend's hand on his shoulder still made him jump.

"How did you know where to find me?"

Taste of Revenge

"I followed yer scrawny ass as soon as I saw ye take off." Alastor clapped his hand on his back. "We'll find her, mate."

"She's not here. I can't feel her."

"They used yer love for her against ye. Knew ye'd run blindly after her. They're cunning bastards."

"Where do you think they took her?"

"Where else? The forest."

"Fuck." Gareth kicked over a chair. It had taken the Van Wildens, even with their help, ages to find the Forest Clan lair the first time. Now they had to find them again?

"We have to tell Mr. and Mrs. V. They'll wanna find her, too."

Gareth nodded.

"Four sets of eyes and ears are better than two."

Gareth sighed. "Yeah, you're right."

Alastor clapped him again on the shoulder. "Aye, that I am."

Gareth's top lip curled up. He was not in the mood to laugh.

CHAPTER 18

Morgana opened her eyes, taking in her surroundings. She was at the location of the abandoned Forest lair site, which was also where Mariza's wild-rose cage ring-of-death had been.

Her eyes narrowed as she saw the remaining huts Mariza hadn't destroyed that were once nestled amongst the canopy of the trees now scattered haphazardly surrounding her. Some were barely standing. A strong gust of wind could easily knock them right over.

The Forest Clan went from living in the treetops to the town lair to residing on the ground. If they weren't going to be eradicated by her and her family soon, she might wonder where they'd try to live next.

It was a very bold move for Ragnorok to have his lair out in the open like this. But as far as she was aware, the humans stayed out of the forest nowadays. And this was the furthest section of the forest from Oak Wood Hills. *Clever*.

Morgana looked to her left and right, a small gasp escaping her mouth.

She wasn't the only one strapped to a pole. But unlike her, these humans were only tied to theirs by rope. She had silver chains snaking around her torso, strapping her to the pole, biting into the exposed flesh from her bullet wounds.

They had stripped off her jacket, her dark gray tank top remained, leaving her with some modesty. Her leather pants had been rolled up to her knees, her bare arms pinned to her sides.

She needed to be free of these chains. There was no way she was going to stick around and be a part of whatever sick and twisted plot Ragnorok had cooked up. She looked around. Her mind raced with different possibilities until she settled on one.

If she broke one of her limbs or hands, the ties would no longer bind them.

Morgana could do it. She could break her arm or dislocate her shoulder to slip from the chains. It was only the burning sensation she had to withstand, but she could do this. She was Morgana-freakin'-Van Wilden. She took down large vampire clans like this all the time.

What was a little debilitating silver poisoning?

She breathed in deep and psyched herself up. *Okay, it's just pain. Pain is freedom. You've got to suffer a bit of it to get out of here. You can do this.*

She gritted her teeth and dislocated her shoulder. She'd bitten down on her tongue to stop herself from calling out, and now she could taste her blood.

She swirled it around in her mouth and shrugged—not quite sure what the big deal was about the taste.

She shimmied her arm through the chains, grinding her teeth as the silver scraped her skin, leaving large purple-red welts. Tears gathered in her eyes. Oh, how she wanted to cry out. She ground her teeth, determined to do this. Inch by painful inch, her arms were finally freed. Gritting her teeth, she pushed her shoulder back into place, holding in her scream. Once the feeling had returned to that arm, she shoved the chains down around her legs, drawing a sharp intake of breath as the chains fell around her ankles. She quickly glanced around before racing away from the pole. The exertion of running and the silver poisoning slowed her down. Her chest heaved as she dropped to her hands and knees.

Morgana crawled along the ground, trying to put as much distance between them. She groaned inward when she felt a vampire standing over her. *Oh, shit.*

Taste of Revenge

He yanked at her hair, dragging her upward.

She bit back the cry at the pain in her scalp.

"Going somewhere?" he sneered. He was wearing a leather vest, and his muscular arms were bare. From the look of his hairstyle—shaved down the sides with a short mohawk on top—this vampire was old, but she also sensed it from his presence.

Dammit.

The vampire dragged her back by her hair, pain radiating in her scalp. She clawed at his hand to free herself. He threw her up against the pole, a spasm spreading across her back from the force. Another vampire wrapped the silver chains back around her—this time intertwining and winding them tighter.

The vampire who'd caught her tapped the pistol on her chest, right where her heart was. "I think I should put a bullet right in here for that, stop you from escaping again."

"Do you even know how to use that thing? You look like you came from the Viking era," Morgana said snidely to mask her fear, but even she could hear her heart hammering against her ribcage. Being the only Dhampir, there was no way to know if a silver bullet to the heart would kill her. And she didn't want to test it.

Ragnorok appeared and placed a hand on the vampire's hand holding the gun.

"What are you doing? We want her alive. Who knows what a silver bullet would do to her heart. We want to harvest her blood, do we not?"

Viking vampire pulled the gun away. "Sorry, boss."

If she weren't being held up by chains, Morgana would have sagged with relief at the threat of her life being taken away. "Always the pretty ones who are dumb," she spoke, feigning bravado.

Viking vampire bared his fangs.

Morgana raised her eyebrows.

Ragnorok shook his head and held out his hand.

The vampire begrudgingly handed over the gun.

The Forest Clan leader then aimed the gun at Morgana's left shoulder and began unloading bullets into various parts of her body.

Morgana ground her teeth, muffling the howls wanting to escape from her throat. The bullets exacerbated the pain throughout her body. How could she endure even more? Her breathing haggard, her head fell forward.

Ragnorok placed his hand on her cheek, tilting her head to look into her the eyes.

She tried to convey as much hatred toward him as she could.

He smiled and spoke to the Viking, "Besides what I have planned for her, I want her to feel this. She has to live."

"Fuck you," she rasped.

"But I thought—" her captor protested.

Ragnorok dropped his hand, letting her face fall back down. He turned to the vampire. "Don't think. Just do what I say."

"Yes, Ragnorok." The vampire bowed his head.

Ragnorok shook his head, turning back to Morgana. "Barbarians some of them. All about the kill, kill, kill. Never about savoring the moment. The slow, torturous deaths are always the best." He shook his head and waved at her. "And make sure she's chained tight. We don't want her escaping again."

CHAPTER 19

Alastor watched his friend slump forward onto his knees, a cry escaping his lips before he fell into silence.

Oscar and Vivienne arrived at the town lair shortly after.

"Perhaps I should take him back to the house?" Vivienne crouched down, looking concerned at Gareth.

"No." Gareth tried to stand, pushing her away from him. "I need to find her."

"Calm yourself, son. You're too volatile now. Alastor can search the town lair for any clues to their whereabouts. I'll look for any evidence outside our home."

"No," Gareth protested.

Oscar planted a firm hand on his shoulder. "Go back to the house. Take a moment to calm yourself."

Oscar gazed into Gareth's eyes. "You're letting your emotions block any other feelings."

Realization dawned on his best friend's face, "You mean—"

Oscar nodded. "Your bond. It should lead us straight to her. But your emotions are overpowering anything you might be feeling from her."

Gareth looked at Alastor, who nodded.

Vivienne placed an arm around his shoulders, leading him away.

"Go inside the house, Alastor, and try to find anything that will lead us to her." Oscar didn't quite meet his eyes.

"Aye." His brow furrowed. Why was Oscar acting so strange around him?

Alastor trudged back up the porch steps entering the town lair. The stench of death—old and new blood—made his gums throb and his fangs lengthen while his stomach heaved. He followed this foul mixture of scents until he came across a large metal door. A bookshelf was shoved to the side. Pushing his way inside, the scene that met him was like something out of one of those horror movies Ava made him sit through. Even though half the time she never ended up watching it, her face was buried in his chest throughout most of the movie. He shook his head and muttered, "Jaysus-Mary-feckin'-Christ."

Brown blood stains lined the walls of the empty room. Hanging from the ceilings were some sort of bindings also caked in dried blood. *What the feck where they doing in here?*

If the human police saw this, then they'd be asking *a lot* of questions. Now that he was an agent of The Council, this was something they needed to avoid. They'd been doing a good job of keeping the local police away from the actions of the Forest Clan.

But what was he to do with this mess?

If he were with Morgana, she would know what to do.

"But she ain't here, ye feckin' eejit."

Shuddering, he decided to hightail it out of there quickly and go report this to the others.

CHAPTER 20

Every now and then, Morgana would grit her teeth, mustering the little strength that wasn't draining from her body and tried to shift forward.

She never moved.

Then she tried to send feelings through the bond, but it felt like trying to push jelly through a sieve.

She gazed down at her body. Blood oozed out of the bullet wounds from her stomach and shoulder, dripping down her body into a child's shallow plastic pool, gathering around her feet like the autumn leaves had. To add more insult, they'd slashed her wrists along the veins and vampires were approaching with plastic cups as if she were some goddamn fountain of youth.

Every now and then a vampire would be even cruder and lap up her fallen blood directly from the kiddie pool like an animal.

She gritted her teeth and tried to struggle against the chains whenever they did this, the worst of them being Ragnorok.

The first time he grabbed her wrist, Morgana struggled to wrench her limb free, and he cut into her skin with a silver knife. That wound would remain open until she ingested vampire blood from someone who loved her. It was a strange vampire lore—no one knew from whence it came—but it was the only way to heal silver poisoning.

Ragnorok pressing his fingers into the cut, drew her from her thoughts and a hiss from her lips. The blood oozed out more rapidly than her other wounds. He snapped his fingers, and a gangly looking vampire hurried up with a silver goblet in hand. Ragnorok held the cup underneath this new cut and collected the blood flowing from it.

He brought the goblet to his lips, never breaking eye contact with Morgana who grunted and struggled against the chains, slurping up her blood rather noisily.

"Ah, simply divine." He smacked his lips and raised the goblet as if to toast her. "Your blood is indeed special, isn't it? The human blood enriched with vampire blood. Delicious and satisfying, giving vampires extra strength. Simply marvelous. Exactly what I need for my people."

"I'm not a fucking living blood bag, you bastard."

"Who said anything about keeping you alive?"

"Once all your blood is gone, you will starve like a normal vampire. It's going to be quite painful." He gave her a wicked smile.

Morgana had never heard of a Primus starving to death, but then again, they'd never wanted for blood. Thinking of her family steeled her spine. "My family will come and get me."

"Oh, I'm banking on that." He turned to face her. "You see, I'm going to destroy you and your whole fucking family. And that will trigger a war with The Council."

"You won't be able to kill them."

"Ah, but I will. Because you will tell me the secret to killing the Primus Vampyr."

"Like hell, I will."

"Then I'll just have to make you tell me." He pushed one of the bullets in her arm further into her flesh, causing her to cry out, her screams ringing in the air.

"Fuck you!"

Ragnorok threw his head back and laughed. "No *thank you,* my dear, contrary to belief, we're not animals. Why would anyone want to fuck a cow?"

"A cow?"

"You *are* being 'milked' for your blood, are you not?"

"Once I get out of these chains, your ass is as good as ash." She gritted.

"We shall see, shall we?"

CHAPTER 21

Where was she?

The question echoed in Gareth's mind. He held his head in his hands. How strange it was to be alone with his emotions. He was so used to feeling what Morgana felt wrapped around his own. There was a sense of comfort knowing where Morgana was at all times—all gone now, vanished in one moment. His still, un-beating heart twisted with emotion at the thought of not seeing his mate again, of not being able to hold her, feel her, and taste her lips again. The only other time he felt pain this immense was the night he'd been turned and left to rot as he starved to death. But this pain was born from the heart and his mind—a far more powerful pain.

The smell of blood wafted toward his nose as a glass of blood was being held near his face. He shook his head.

Taste of Revenge

"Gareth, dear, you need to eat," Vivienne coaxed.

"I'm not hungry." He shoved the glass away from his face, not caring if any blood spilled on the rug.

A firm grip lifted his chin, and he met the icy-blue eyes—not of the doting motherly figure he and Alastor affectionately dubbed Mrs. V, but the hardened stare of the drill sergeant who whooped their asses in training. "Eat, Gareth. You will not do her any good once we find her if you're half-starved and weakened by this ordeal," she snarled.

Gareth snatched the glass of blood out of her hands, never breaking eye contact with her as he drained the contents. "Did you learn that look from Oscar?" he muttered, passing the tumbler back to her, then wiped his mouth with the back of his hand.

Vivienne's lips twitched. "I'll get you more."

Gareth nodded and dropped his head. A firm hand on his shoulder made him look up at Vivienne once more, this time she was looking at him with care and empathy. "We'll find her. I want her home safe as much as you do."

Gosh, he was a bastard. Here he was wallowing in his own grief when Vivienne was probably sick with worry herself but was forcing him to eat. He couldn't fathom how a parent would feel about their missing child. "I'm sorry, Mrs. V, about before."

She smiled at him. "Don't you worry about me. I'm tough."

Oscar chose that moment to stride in through the front door. Brutus was wagging his tail at his master's return as he ran up to him. Oscar absentmindedly bent down and scratched him behind the ears with his left hand. His right hand curled tightly into a fist. Oscar walked over to them and opened his hand to reveal bullet casings, confirming what Gareth instinctively knew.

"I found these outside. Silver bullets."

The sound of wood splintering reached their ears. Gareth turned to see Vivienne's hands had crushed the armrests. "He shot her with silver bullets?" Her fingers dug deeper into the chair, which happened to be Oscar's favorite armchair.

"Yes, my dear. Could you please refrain from breaking my chair?"

Vivienne stood, her icy-blue eyes blazing. "I don't care about your armchair. Our daughter is out there weakened from the silver."

"And we'll find her," Oscar bellowed. Brutus barked along with him. "We'll use every weapon, every resource, every tracking skill we possess. We must find her."

Vivienne withdrew her hands, glancing down at the splinters embedded in her skin. "Oscar Van Wilden, don't you yell at me. We're all upset. But right now, we need to band together not fall apart." She closed her eyes and opened them, calmer. "We all need to strategize with a clear mind."

"I'm not just upset. I am furious. *That monster has my daughter.*"

"And we'll get her back. I know this is difficult for you when it's only been a couple of weeks since the other one's passing."

Oscar's eyebrows furrowed. "The other one." He paused. "Oh yes, Mariza." He pulled at his collar.

Vivienne crossed her arms over chest, her face wincing. Oscar strode over to her and kneeled, pulling her arms away from her chest and looked down at her hands. "These need to come out, dear." He began plucking the splinters out with his fingernails, eliciting hisses from Vivienne's lips.

Her eyes looked stormy as she looked up at her husband, her tone bitter, "She's not really dead, is she?"

Gareth looked up, his head swiveling between the two of them. "Who's not really dead?"

"Mariza." Vivienne hissed through clenched teeth.

"What?" Gareth leaped to his feet.

Oscar sighed, looking toward the ceiling. "No, she's not."

Vivienne's eyes narrowed. She stood. "I knew you were hiding something."

Oscar's eyes widened.

"You didn't know that I know about your ability to hide things within our bond, did you?"

Oscar rubbed the back of his neck. "How long have you known?"

"Since the first time you did it."

"Where *is she,* then?" Gareth asked, not believing what he was hearing.

"She's been imprisoned," Oscar replied.

"For how long?" Vivienne asked.

"One hundred years."

"A hundred years," Vivienne screeched.

"Think about it, dear, you'll be five hundred by then. Your strength will be quite superior."

"I don't care about her coming after me again. It's the fact you lied to me, Oscar Van Wilden."

"Jesus, what is with you Van Wildens and keeping secrets," Gareth muttered.

Oscar looked over at Gareth, his brown eyes boring into his. "I'll choose to ignore that comment for now as you're upset over Morgana."

Gareth grimaced. "I didn't mean any disrespect."

Oscar nodded. "Very well. But it's the nature of the beast. If you've lived your whole life keeping your true existence a secret, then, of course, you harbor other secrets as well."

"And what of my question?" Vivienne asked.

"What question is that, my dear?"

"Why did you lie to us about keeping Mariza alive?"

"I told you before I'll not see any of my children die. So, we need to move past this and go rescue my other daughter." He turned to Vivienne. "Our daughter."

"Very well." Vivienne sat back down, her lips thinning as she straightened her skirt over her thighs. "We'll put this issue aside to rescue Morgana. For now. But do *not* think I'll forget about this."

"You wouldn't be the woman I married if you did."

"All this tension. Morgana's capture. It's all my fault." Gareth held his head in his hands.

"No, son." Oscar placed his hand on Gareth's shoulder. "If we're playing the blame game, then I'd also have to shoulder that as well. I wasn't fast enough despite my age. I couldn't get to her in time. I felt them coming. I should have gone around the front of the house first."

"No dear, you were arming yourself. If anyone is to blame, it is Ragnorok." Vivienne's eyes took on a deathly look. "We all know Morgana was capable of going out there on her own."

"But not when Ragnorok knew about her silver poisoning," Gareth protested. "I should have been out there with her."

"You know Morgana would have rolled her eyes at you and still insisted she go out on her own."

"I know, but—"

Oscar grabbed Gareth's shoulders. "Look at me," he demanded.

Gareth grunted and forced himself to look into Oscar's eyes. Something he didn't want to do because they reminded him so much of Morgana's. "But what if he has killed her already?"

"You would have felt it."

Gareth narrowed his eyes.

"The bond can only be broken in death," Oscar explained.

"But I can't feel her now."

"Then I can only assume she's been weakened quite severely or she's unconscious. Trust me, you would have felt like half of your soul and heart had been ripped right out of your body." Oscar's face fell. It was the first time Gareth had heard of him talking about his first wife's death.

"Is that what you felt?"

"Yes," Oscar replied, looking down at his empty hands. Gareth found it odd he wasn't holding a tumbler full of whiskey. "I'll tell you what it was like."

CHAPTER 22

Four Thousand Years Ago...

Octavius stood in the trench that had been dug around the outskirts of their hometown. What the Primus had affectionately dubbed *the village* because none of the Elders could come up with a name they all agreed upon. All had been happy in the village until war had reached their streets only a fortnight ago. Octavius was arguing with Batheras, their unofficial leader, about the latest battle strategy to take place.

A group was to head around the back of the oncoming horde of human-turned vampires who were lusting for blood. Whether it be their blood or the few remaining humans the Primus were trying to protect, Octavius wasn't sure.

His wife, Delizera, was to be among that group. Octavius didn't like the idea of his wife fighting.

Their daughter, Mariza, had volunteered to remain behind in the safehold of the village with the children and grandchildren of the other Primus. His two sons were fighting Dieter Dovkosky and his band of human-turned vampires in another sector.

He didn't want to lose anyone, so he was trying to convince his wife to stay behind with Mariza. But Delizera was stubborn as the day was long. She would not hear any more talk of her staying behind. His wife stood tall at six feet, five inches. The extra height allowed her to tower over him, glowering at him. Her long blonde hair that usually fell loosely to her waist was now braided along the sides of her head and pulled back, tied by a leather strap. She'd also changed out of her long flowing dress into cowhide breeches and a vest. She looked quite the formidable warrior. His attire was a similar fashion. His long dark hair was swept back and tied at his nape to avoid flying in his face when fighting.

"Octavius, this is the future of our children we have to protect."

Octavius sighed. He knew better than anyone not to argue with her. "Very well, but be careful, my love."

Delizera smiled and pressed her lips to his. "Aren't I always, dear husband?"

He chuckled before she turned, picking up her spear and joining the others in her group.

Taste of Revenge

Oscar sent his love for her through their bond. Delizera paused and turned her head to the side, a smile on her olive face as she sent the same feeling back.

His wife was tough. She would be safe.

Octavius strode with Batheras through the trenches listening to the other Elder relay the latest news from the enemy camp.

"Truly, it has been a terrible mess, letting their family squabbles spill into war like this," Batheras complained.

Octavius agreed. Ion Dovkosky was a proud man, this would no doubt be a blow to his pride.

As they marched along, a pain speared Octavius' heart. He stopped, gripping Batheras' arm, his other hand clutched at his stomach, then moved to his chest. Something was not right with his wife.

He'd felt her feelings of fear but had pushed them to the back of his mind as he discussed war tactics with Batheras. Now there was something like a wall had been slammed down on their bond, shutting him out.

An emptiness unlike anything he had felt before, engulfed him. Like an endless black void had swallowed half his being, he felt soulless.

"What's wrong, my friend?" Batheras reached out to steady him when he lost his step. The blood drained from his face as he turned to his friend. "Delizera. I don't feel her."

Agnor's eldest son, Endre, came running, huffing, and panting, grasping his knees as he caught his breath. Blood had become scarce since the war started—many of the Primus, not having fed for days, were left weaker than usual.

"Elder Octavius, you must come quickly. It's Delizera, she has fallen in battle."

Octavius turned to Batheras. "Send word to my children."

He followed the young vampire to the edge of the battlefield where the surviving Primus had dragged several of their fallen comrades' bodies.

Endre led him to where Agnor and Ohana were kneeling over his wife's body. She was laid out over the grass and fallen leaves. Her blue-green eyes were closed. He would never be able to look into those depths again. Pain ripped through his heart like someone had reached inside his chest, taken hold of it and was shredding it in their hands.

"No. No. It can't be," he cried.

Two twisted branches were protruding from her stomach and chest. The scent of hawthorn invaded his nostrils. He always knew something about the trees that grew in the neighboring forests wasn't quite right. He'd always had an instinctual feeling to stay away from them. Now he knew why. From the way her body was not healing or reviving, hawthorn was lethal to the Primus.

Agnor withdrew each of the branches, passing one onto Ohana, holding the other one up. The ends were coated in his wife's blood, but he was still able to see the crudely carved pointed ends. "Looks like they've found a way to kill us."

Oscar wasn't listening as he fell to his knees. "No. No, not my Delizera." He scooped her body up, cradling her close, not caring if her blood coated him.

The presence of his children arrived, tugging at his heart more. He shouldn't have sent for them. They shouldn't see their mother like this.

"Mother!" Mariza cried, dropping to her side, taking hold of her cold hand.

Hector crouched next to him. All traces of his humorous nature were absent from his features. "Who did this?" he growled.

Jonas stood by his sister's side, squeezing her shoulder. She looked up at him, tearfully. He crouched down, holding her close as she cried on his shoulder.

"Unfortunately, she's not the only one." Batheras placed his hand on Octavius' shoulder. He glanced around at the other Primus gathering by their fallen loved ones. But right now, all he cared about was his wife, the wife he would never see again.

CHAPTER 23

The Present...

Gareth glanced between Oscar and Vivienne, gauging their reactions to Oscar's tale.

The Elder was staring into the unlit fireplace. Brutus nuzzled at his hand. Oscar's voice was monotone. "It's not a feeling you forget in a hurry... that immense loss, overwhelming you, suffocating you. The emotions you once shared, now gone, an empty void suffocating you as you try to breathe." Oscar looked up at him, his once bright, rich brown eyes had become dull, his face slack. "When you feel that, then you can wallow in your grief. But for now, we *don't* give up hope. She's alive, and we will get her back."

Vivienne looked like she'd sucked a lemon during her husband's memory of his first and lost love.

Taste of Revenge

Gareth empathized with her. It's not easy hearing about one's first love. Hell, Morgana had slapped him when she found out about Mariza, but that could have also been the fact he compared her to his evil creator.

After a moment or two of awkward silence, Vivienne's face softened. She reached out for Oscar's hand. "She was a great woman."

Oscar looked up with sadness still dulling his brown eyes, but an expression of appreciation filled his face with warmth. He withdrew his hand from hers and touched her cheek. "She *was* a great woman. I loved her dearly. She gave me three beautiful children. But she's my past. You, my dear, are my present and future." Vivienne closed her eyes, leaning into his touch.

Gareth tore his own eyes away. His heart ached to touch Morgana again. He looked to the ceiling, whispering thanks when he felt Alastor approaching the house.

Oscar and Vivienne pulled apart, sharing a small smile before their attention was on Brutus. The large puppy scurried over to the door. He stumbled as he was still not used to his oversized paws. He bumped into a table as the vase on top wobbled. Vivienne was there in a flash catching the porcelain before it smashed onto the floor.

"Maybe you should dog-proof the house," Gareth suggested.

"It's fine." Vivienne straightened the vase. "I can just run after him to catch things."

"You know he's going to get spoiled doing it that way."

Vivienne shrugged. "I never got to have any more children. He can be like my second child."

"You mean like what the humans call fur babies?"

"Exactly. Oscar likes to act human, why can't I do the same? After all, I *was* a human."

Alastor walked in, interrupting their conversation.

Brutus jumped and yapped at his ankles.

"Ah good, Alastor, you're here. What did you find?" Oscar was all business again.

Alastor looked grimly at them all, recounting what he'd found in the old town lair.

Gareth's lip curled. "Way to perpetuate the stereotypes of all vampires being evil monsters."

"Well, the Night Dwellers were the ones who inspired the human stories," said Vivienne, her face looking rather sickly.

Gareth stood. "I hope that's not what they're going to do to Morgana. You know she'd hate that shit."

Oscar and Vivienne exchanged grim looks.

"We don't know for sure, but…" Vivienne's eyes dropped to her hands.

Oscar patted her hand, which had healed completely from the splinters. "We'll get her back, dear." He turned back to them. "That would explain how we couldn't enter the town lair before. The humans they kept there were still living. And they would have swapped them out long before the protection fell. Explains why they were taking so many people." Oscar scrubbed his face before standing and walking over to the mantelpiece. He leaned against it, his arm propped on the shelf. Brutus looked up at him with sad, large brown eyes. He wasn't entirely joking before when he had told Gareth the two of them shared a special bond. It was like the dog could see into his soul sometimes. Brutus nudged his leg with his nose—an attempt to cheer up his master.

"Thanks, buddy, but it's not going to work this time," he said quietly, "I miss your—" He had almost said *sister* to Brutus, who was now tilting his head. The puppy knew more than he let on.

Alastor waited patiently for Oscar to finish his orders. His voice had trailed off, and the Elder was absentmindedly scratching Brutus behind the ears while staring at the far wall.

During Randalf's fight with Morgana, there had been some damage done to the living room walls, and even though the repairs were done well, they could all see the difference in the dark wood panels—the new ones were slightly lighter. That night, Morgana had Gareth there to help her, while Oscar, Vivienne, and eventually Alastor had all been knocked out, unable to help her. And now she was in trouble again, and none of them were around to help her this time either. It had to gnaw at a fellow, especially her parent.

Alastor exchanged a look with the others before deciding to speak. "Aye, what are we goin' to do about it, then?"

Oscar turned to him. "Usually, I'd say we should go out and clean it up before the human authorities catch wind of it. But with Morgana missing—" his voice strained, his eyes full of pain.

Vivienne stood, walking over to him. "Didn't you say that area wasn't to be developed for another week?"

He nodded.

Vivienne patted his arm, leaning closer, her voice barely audible to him and Alastor. "I know, dear, I know." In a much louder voice, she spoke to them both, "Then we have a few days to find Morgana and end the Forest Clan. Plus, a couple of days to clean up the 'mess' like we do after every mission. But we need to get started straightaway."

The light in Oscar's eyes brightened, and he pulled his shoulders back. "As always, you're right, my dear." He smiled warmly to his wife before turning to Gareth and Alastor. "What do we know so far?"

"Well, the town lair has been abandoned," Gareth replied.

"Do ye think they've gone back to the forest?" Alastor asked.

Gareth shook his head. "Nah, Mariza destroyed that place to build her death ring."

"Aye." Alastor shifted, rubbing the back of his neck and looking up at Oscar.

Oscar's eyes were once again averted as he pulled at his collar.

Gareth groaned inward. *Shit, Alastor still didn't know*. He opened his mouth to say something to his best friend, but Vivienne placed her hand on his arm, shaking her head. "Let Oscar do it."

"Let Mr. V do what?" Alastor's eyebrow raised.

Oscar cleared his throat. "Alastor, there's something you must know," he looked down at his whiskey glass, "... about when you staked Mariza."

"Killed, don't ye mean?" His head snapped up.

"Ah, no. Mariza is still alive. She's being held at Headquarters in a prisoner containment cell."

"Feck." Alastor scrubbed at his face. "So, I never killed her?" He stood, pointing his finger. "How is that feckin' possible?"

Oscar cleared his throat again. "I had switched Morgana's hawthorn stakes with fake ones."

"Fuck," Gareth muttered.

"Did ye know?" his friend turned to him, his green eyes blazing.

Gareth put his palms up, shaking his head. "I only just found out just before you got here."

"I'm sorry for deceiving you all." Oscar looked down at his glass.

Alastor stood, an urge to run downstairs and lay a few hits on the wooden training dummy. "I hope ye don't mind, but I might sit this one out tonight."

Gareth raised an eyebrow. "You won't go with us to search for Morgana?"

Alastor sighed at the wounded look in his best friend's eyes. There was more to worry about than him going off to lick his wounded pride. His best friend needed him. Alastor sat back down. "Aye, I'll go." He stared into the unlit fireplace unable to look at Oscar. All those times he had felt guilty about killing the Elder's daughter. The truth was dawning on him why Oscar had *really* been uncomfortable around him. That gave him a small amount of comfort.

Vivienne squeezed his shoulder, but he shrugged her off.

"So, what about the caves?" Oscar asked. "Ragnorok's first clan, the Obscure Clan, lived in an underground network of caves. You boys have both lived here a long time. Do you know of any local caves?"

"Nay, but Ava might," Alastor mumbled.

Taste of Revenge

"Well, why don't you go see her and find out what she knows?" Vivienne suggested. "And just call us when you do." Vivienne was giving him an out.

"Aye." He stood, scratching Brutus absently on his head before exiting the house and closing the door behind him. He stood there for a moment wanting to gather his thoughts. How could he have been deceived like that? He was proud of that kill, albeit a little guilty when he was around Oscar.

Brutus whined, scratching at the door.

"What's wrong, Brutus?" Vivienne cooed from inside.

"He probably senses Alastor's mood," Oscar mumbled.

"I should go talk to him," Gareth's voice filtered through the walls.

"No, let me," Vivienne spoke softly.

Alastor stomped across the front porch, not wanting to hear what they had to say. Vivienne was approaching him, and her hand reached out to stop him. "Alastor, wait. Please don't be too mad at Oscar," Vivienne said gently. "He loves his children. He would do anything for them."

"What about, ye? He deceived ye, too."

"I knew he was hiding something that day." Vivienne smiled.

He recognized her fake smile. She used it a lot during the public events on Oscar's campaign trail.

"And yer okay with him lying to us about that?"

"No. Once this is all over, he's in the doghouse. With Brutus. But right now, we need to worry about my daughter and getting her home safe."

Alastor rubbed the back of his neck. "Aye. I just don't like all the deception."

Vivienne chuckled, though it was hollow. "That's what Gareth said."

Alastor gave her a grim smile. "Well, if Gareth can still stand to be around Oscar, then I should be able to."

"So, you will come along and help us look for her?" Her icy-blue eyes were big and round.

"Aye. I'd never let Morgana down. She's become one of me best mates, too. Just let me talk to the missus first."

"Thank you, Alastor."

"Aye." Alastor nodded as he walked off. He could have phoned Ava, but he needed space from the Van Wildens right now, and he knew Ava's comforting touch would set him straight.

CHAPTER 24

Alastor let himself into Ava's darkened apartment. The only light came from the glow of the flat-screen television. Ava's back was facing him.

"Babe, is that you?" She turned her head to the side.

"Aye," he answered grimly.

She lifted the remote and paused the movie playing, concern etched on her face as she shifted her position to face him. "What's going on?"

Alastor sunk into the sofa, closing his eyes, leaning his head against the back of the green couch. "What do ye know about any caves around here?"

Ava's limbs brushed his body as she snuggled up next to him. He opened his eyes to look at her. Her head tilted to the side, and she had that faraway look in her hazel eyes she got whenever she was thinking. "Well, there's the Lost World Caverns nearby. But they're too much of a tourist draw... not somewhere for vampires to discreetly hide out. Plenty of food sources, sure, but people would notice all the tourists going missing. But that would also play into Ragnorok's hands from what I understand.

"There are supposed to be large limestone formations further out consisting of miles of underground caves. Maybe check them out? Or have you tried the waterfalls?"

"Aye, thanks. I'll pass the details on."

Ava touched his knee. "What's going on, Alastor? You seem a little dreary."

Alastor sighed. "Turns out I didn't kill Mariza after all."

Ava furrowed her brow. "No?"

"No."

She pulled him to her chest, resting her chin on top of his head. "I know how much that kill meant to you."

Alastor snuggled into her chest. If there were one place a man could garner comfort from, it was a woman's bosom.

"Ye don't sound too surprised to hear that, love."

"After what we've dealt with for the last few months, nothing about what the Van Wildens do surprises me anymore."

Alastor stretched out along her sofa, pulling her down to lay on top of him. She placed her cheek to his chest.

"Ava, love?"

"Mmm?" She snuggled into him.

"I love ye."

She lifted her head and rested her chin on top of her hands and looked at him. "I love you, too." She smiled at him, and he returned the gesture.

"The both of us... together forever." He stroked her blonde hair.

"Of course." She laid her head back onto his chest, and he continued to stroke her hair. "So, would you come with me if I got the job in Summerville?"

Alastor's hand froze. He didn't know how to answer. He and Gareth were now part of the Van Wildens. He supposed wherever they went, the two of them would have to go too.

"I think Mrs. V was saying something before this whole thing with Morgana that Gareth and I'll be goin' back with them to HQ to be initiated properly as agents."

"Ah, okay."

"But ye could come with us? Ye haven't had a proper holiday in years. Not since I've met ye."

"That's true. But what if I get the job, and they want me to start straightaway?"

"Then maybe I could ask to be assigned back here to be near ye. We'll work something out."

Ava lifted her head and looked at him again, smiling. "That sounds good."

"Aye, it does." He smiled back at her.

Ava giggled and squirmed, her hips moving against his.

"Oi, stop, lass, you'll make me hard doin' that."

"Oh, sorry. I didn't mean to… doesn't feel right to do it while Morgana is captured."

"Aye, I know." Alastor brushed her hair back off her face. "I'm all right like this."

Ava shifted forward and kissed his lips briefly, then pulled back gazing into his eyes.

Alastor lifted his head and kissed her again before laying back down.

"Just kissing?"

He kissed her again. "Aye, just kissing."

"I like kissing."

"Aye, me, too."

Ava pressed her warm center against him, making his penis press painfully against his fly. She licked her lips before pressing them against his again.

"Oh, feck it. Life's too short."

Ava giggled. "My life, you mean?" She slid her hand under his shirt, trailing down his abs and under his waistband.

"Aye, so we should make the most of it."

She lowered her face to his. "You know if we just do a bit of foreplay, technically we're not fully doing it."

"Aye." His hands slid down her back and into the back of her jeans and underneath her cotton panties, grasping her bare ass. "But ye know we should get the fucking out of the way," mimicking Morgana's earlier words.

Ava giggled. "I thought we already did that?"

Alastor's eyes closed, and he let his head fall back. "Nay, ye can never fuck too many times." His hands withdrew from her pants, and she shifted to the side of him, sliding his zipper down, pulling his hardened shaft out. Her hand wrapped around his cock, sliding up and down with slow, deliberate strokes.

"Aye, love… that's it."

She hummed, rubbing the pad of her thumb along the underside of his head at the sensitive part.

"Jaysus," he moaned. Not wanting to be selfish, he turned onto his side and dipped his hand under the waistband of her jeans again brushing his fingers over the cotton of her panties until he touched her core. "Yer sodden, love."

"Uh-huh." Ava's eyes were half-lidded as she continued to stroke. "What can I say, you turn me on, Irish."

He chuckled before delving his hand in deeper and pushing aside the material stroking a finger through her wet folds. Ava groaned, her strokes picking up speed. He pushed his finger inside her opening.

"Yes," Ava hissed. He swirled it around, teasing her. "More," she groaned.

"Like this?" He inserted another finger, pushing in as far as he could with her jeans restricting his movements. Her hand moved faster, and the familiar tingle in his balls meant his impending release.

"Nay, I need to be inside ye, lass." He withdrew his hands, took her hand off his penis, and flipped her onto her back, making her squeal.

"Why did you take our hands away?" she frowned.

Instead of replying, he unzipped her jeans, grabbing the waistband of both her pants and underwear, yanking them down her legs and flinging them across the room. He lifted her legs over his shoulders and sheathed himself inside.

"That's a good reason!" Ava cried, her insides clenching him as he thrust his hips harder into her.

"That's it, love… come for me."

She shuddered underneath him, wetness coating him. He withdrew and plunged deeper, his balls smacking her ass.

"Harder, Alastor," Ava panted.

"I can't, love," he huffed, his eyes screwed shut. He was already thrusting into her as fast as he safely could.

"Harder." She slapped her palm on top of the green sofa cushions.

"Nay, love, anymore, and I'll hurt ye."

"I can take it. Please, I need it harder and faster," she growled.

"Not unless yer a vampire, ye can't."

"But I don't want to be a vampire," she cried out in frustration arching her back.

Alastor stilled. "What did ye say?"

Ava opened her eyes wide and lifted her head to look at him. "I mean… well, of course, I do."

"But ye just said ye didn't." He pulled out of her and stood, tucking himself back into his trousers and zipping up his fly. This was not a conversation to be had with his wee fella hanging out.

Ava turned on the sofa and reached her arm out to him. "You know I do. Just not right now."

"Aye, but just now ye said ye don't want to be a vampire. Full stop."

Ava sat up. "I just enjoy being a human, okay? I don't want to get into the whole blood-sucking thing right now."

"Aye, I get that. And I never wanted ye to feel obligated to become what I am. I just thought ye said ye wanted to. Someday."

Ava rubbed her arm. "I do… eventually. With the Van Wildens here, I toyed with the possibility of doing it sooner. But with the Summerville job coming up, I just thought I'd remain human for a bit longer."

"I understand all that. And ye know ye could still be a vampire and do all that. It's what Gareth and I have been doing for years."

"I know, but now I'm thinking, if I became a vampire now, then I'd miss out on opportunities like that. Won't I be all like rah, rah? I von to suck your blood." She did a poor Transylvanian accent and made her hands into claws and moved them next to her face.

Alastor bit his lips, wanting to laugh despite being angry. "Aye, at the start—"

"See, that's my point. By the time I'm able to be around humans, it'll be harder to crack into those journalism jobs. You've got to really work your way up."

"I understand, love. But ye made it sound like it was never goin' to happen."

"I didn't mean to sound like that," she said softly.

"Ye know I love ye and will support ye with however ye want to be, but ye have to be honest with me. Do ye truly want to become a vampire or not?"

"Yes. No. I don't know. Eventually." Her face contorted.

Alastor's face softened. He leaned over and kissed her forehead. "I'm going to go and leave ye to think about it on yer own."

"Wait, we can still talk about this together."

"Nay. Ye need to make the decision on yer own. Either way, I'll still love ye."

"Okay," she said in a small voice.

"I have to get back to the Van Wildens, anyway." He walked over to her apartment door, placing his hand on the knob before pausing. He turned back around. "Don't go out unless one of us is with ye, okay?"

"Of course."

"Goodbye, love." He grinned at her to let her know there were no hard feelings. It was true—whatever she decided, he would accept.

She smiled back at him from her seated position on the couch. "Bye, Alastor."

CHAPTER 25

Alastor showered at his and Gareth's house before changing into a black wool turtleneck and trousers, then headed back to the Van Wildens.

He entered through the front door. Brutus, as usual, was whining and scratching at Alastor to pet him. He obliged the puppy. At first, he had thought it strange the vampire family had adopted a pet, but Brutus was growing on him. He liked the little bugger.

Inside the living room, Gareth and Vivienne were each bent over a laptop.

"Anything?" Vivienne asked, moving her finger over the mousepad.

"Nada." Gareth looked up.

Oscar paced up and down in front of the fireplace, a habit Alastor found the Elder did quite a bit. Only this time he was talking on his phone, a male was on the other end.

"Thank you." Oscar hung up as Alastor took a seat. "Ah, good, Alastor, you're back."

Alastor nodded. He didn't trust himself to speak to Oscar just yet, in case something disrespectful came out of his mouth.

Oscar seemed unperturbed by his silence. "That was the park ranger. He thinks there may be some old caves near a dried-up waterfall, so we'll look there."

"Why didn't you search there when we were looking for the Forest Clan in the first place?" Gareth asked, closing the screen of the laptop.

"Daryll said there must have been a cave there in years gone by, and the entrance is covered up. He only knows about it from old park records. We also didn't consider the caves because we figured Ragnorok would consider that too obvious given the location of his first clan."

"Where about are the caves, dear?" Vivienne interjected.

"Northwest from here."

"That's closer to town than their forest lair was. They could be there."

Oscar nodded. "Get your weapons ready. We're going on a scouting mission."

Downstairs, Alastor and Gareth gathered up stakes, placing them into four holsters. Gareth turned his head to him. "You okay about working with Oscar?"

"Aye." In truth, he had all but forgotten about the Mariza situation after his heated discussion with Ava. He scrubbed his face. "I'll be fine. What I should be askin' is how yer feelin'?"

"The Mariza thing doesn't faze me too much. I've always seen her as something nasty like a cockroach, so it doesn't surprise me she survived like one."

"Nay, I was askin' about Morgana. We haven't had much of a chance to talk."

Gareth grunted, shoving stakes into the leather rather forcefully. "You know I spent my entire vampire existence staying away from relationships with women. Now that I have one, I can't stand being separated from her. Not like this, anyway." He pushed the holster away from him.

"I'd hate to be apart from Ava like that, too."

Gareth clapped him on the back. "Something you two will probably never have to worry about."

"Aye, I hope so." They gathered up the holsters and trudged upstairs, meeting Oscar and Vivienne in the foyer. They had both changed into black trousers and turtlenecks as well. Vivienne's blonde hair was twisted back into a chignon indicating she meant serious business.

Gareth handed them their stake holsters.

"Thank you, Gareth." Oscar belted his.

"Thank you, dear." Vivienne smiled at him.

"Are we all ready?"

He and Gareth nodded.

"Good. Let us proceed."

The four of them ran along the outskirts of the forest keeping their senses open for any stray vampires they might encounter. But all was quiet. It left Alastor feeling uneasy. Was Ragnorok pleased with just taking Morgana? His gut told him the Forest Clan wouldn't be.

They reached the coordinates of the old waterfall. It was now just a small cliff about ten feet high of small gray rock.

"The cave is in there?" Gareth asked, doing a doubletake. "Doesn't look like anyone is using it as a home."

"Could be another entrance." Oscar walked over to a pile of large rocks and began shifting them aside. "We need to explore all our options."

Alastor exchanged a look with Gareth, but he stepped forward with the others helping Oscar.

Soon all the rubble had been cleared, and a wide opening stood before them. It looked like a downturned mouth.

"Doesn't look ominous at all," Gareth said dryly.

They stepped into the cave entrance. Even though they could see inside the cave, it would have been comforting to have brought torches. The smell of dampness and decay invaded his nostrils. There was also a clear lack of vampire presence to be felt.

"We'll just have a quick look around. They could be using wolfsbane plants again." Oscar stepped into the cave mouth.

Alastor raised an eyebrow, exchanging another glance with Gareth. The Council Elder seemed to be on edge and so desperate to find his daughter that he was going to go ahead with exploring this option.

Any residual anger Alastor had felt at Oscar's betrayal and lies faded away. This was a man who would really do anything for his children—even make them all explore vacant caves for a shred of a chance to find one.

Alastor followed without further protest as did the others.

They walked until they saw a split path up ahead. Of course, the path split.

"We'll split up to cover a larger area that way," Oscar ordered.

They all nodded. He and Gareth took the left tunnel, while Oscar and Vivienne took the right.

"I wonder if we'll see any of our distant relatives in here?" Gareth kept his voice low.

"What do ye mean?" Alastor whispered so only Gareth could hear.

Taste of Revenge

"You know, bats."

Alastor chuckled, earning him an elbow to the ribs.

"Keep it quiet. There *could* be vampires in here."

Alastor shook his head but smiled. His best friend was trying to cheer him up.

After exploring miles of empty tunnels and seeing walls of rocks, they both had to concede no one was in here.

They turned back around, heading back the way they came, finding Oscar and Vivienne waiting at the entrance.

"Well, the caves turned out to be a bust," Gareth said. This time, Alastor was the one to elbow him in the ribs. He shook his head at his friend when he began to protest. Oscar was already on edge, no need to aggravate him any further.

"Yes. Let us proceed home, then," Oscar said rather gruffly.

Alastor raised his eyebrows at Gareth and tilted his head toward Oscar as if to silently say *see?*

Gareth nodded, and they all trekked back to the Van Wilden's house.

Even though Gareth had tried to cheer him up before, Alastor could tell his best friend had been disappointed by their lack of findings.

Alastor mentally slapped his forehead. He was an idiot. Instead of Gareth cheering him up, he should have been the one to make his best friend laugh.

Just because Ava didn't know if she wanted to be human or not shouldn't really matter. At least *his girlfriend* was safe and sound. So deep in his thoughts, he didn't realize the others had stopped, and he walked into Gareth's back with a huff.

"What's goin' on 'ere—" His voice died at the sight that met them on the steps of the Van Wilden's home.

CHAPTER 26

Earlier that Night...

The fools.

Ragnorok had his network of human spies watching the Van Wildens for days now, and the so-called trained agents were none the wiser.

The loud, crass pinging noise from one of the human devices made him wince.

Cedric looked up from the thing in his hand. "Tiff says the four of them are on the move."

"Excellent." Ragnorok grinned.

"Do you think this is a good idea, boss?" Nasir asked.

"Yes. I want him to suffer. I want him to feel the burning pain of grief at finding the dead body of a loved one. I want him to feel how I felt finding Svetlana's ashes."

"Why not kill the half-breed, then? Dump her body at their feet?"

"No. Morgana still needs to be alive for what I have planned for her and The Council. No, we move ahead as planned."

"But—" Nasir protested, only to be silenced by Ragnorok's cold stare.

"If you don't have the stomach for this, then I suggest you remain behind. You two…" he pointed to two other wretches, "Come with me." He turned to Cedric. "Send word to your mate that we're to converge on their property. Tell her to go ahead with the next phase."

"Yes, boss." Cedric looked down at the screen, tapping his thumbs on it. While the idea of words magically appearing on the screen fascinated Ragnorok, he missed the days when they had vampire messengers.

Once they were rid of The Council and all the humans were turned, he would ban all human devices.

They were, after all, Night Dwellers, and they were *above* the humans.

Tiffini grimaced at the message on her phone. It wasn't so bad what she had to do.

Taste of Revenge

She looked in the telescope once again checking to see that the house next door remained quiet. Once satisfied, she took the slab of beef leg out of the fridge and held it gingerly in front of her. She walked out of the house a few hundred yards away from the Van Wilden's property and up to their front door.

Taking a deep breath in, she knocked on the door.

The sound of barking could be heard.

After watching the Van Wildens, she knew they never locked their front door. Apparently, they relied on the protection on their home from uninvited vampires. Not uninvited humans. Really, who would be stupid enough to break into a house belonging to vampires? *Her, that's who.*

Placing her free hand on the handle, she turned it, and the door swung inward. Brutus, the name of the dog she'd come to learn during her spying, bounded toward her.

"Hello, little cutie. Remember me?" Every time she'd seen Brutus out with Oscar jogging, she'd made a point of stopping and patting him—all part of the plan to get him to trust her. "Would you like something to eat?" She held the meat out to him. Brutus' tail wagged.

She stepped back from the doorway. "Well, come outside to get it."

Ragnorok arrived at the Van Wilden's property to see Tiffini sitting next to the dog as it happily chewed on their offering. "Good work. You will be rewarded for your efforts," he said to her. She looked toward the dog and nodded slightly.

The dog lifted his paw and growled when he spotted Ragnorok.

Tiffini stood quickly and ran down the front steps.

"Where do you think you're going?" One of the vampires flanking him grabbed her arm.

"My job was to spy and lure the dog out. But I'll not stay and watch what happens next."

"Let her go." Ragnorok waved a hand. *Some vampire she'd make* if she couldn't stomach what was to come. The vampire let her go, and she ran back to the neighboring house.

The dog whined as he watched her go but turned back to Ragnorok, his teeth bared, his hackles raised. Ragnorok smiled. Now he could see the appeal of this creature. But he was not there to admire the beast. He was there for vengeance.

Before the dog could lunge for him, Ragnorok was there grasping the dog's head.

"A message for your master." His grip tightened around the dog's head. Brutus yelped as he twisted.

CHAPTER 27

Back to the Present...

Oscar's stomach twisted at the sight before him. His emotions were still reeling from the memory of Delizera's death. Then to see what was before him, his body shook.

"Jaysus." Alastor turned his head, his chest heaving.

"Fuckin' hell," Gareth muttered. "That fucker's evil."

"Oh no," Vivienne cried, covering her mouth, her shoulders shook with tearless sobs.

But the worst of them was Oscar—a deep guttural cry of agony tore from his lips. He slumped to his knees, crawling along the ground.

Spread across the front porch lay Brutus' forlorn body. A lump of meat and bone next to him. The fading presence of his enemy surrounding them.

No. Not my little buddy. He grasped his hair in his hands.

That fucker was going to pay.

Desperate thoughts shrouded his mind, and Oscar lifted his wrist to his mouth, his fangs piercing his skin. He moved the open cut over Brutus' mouth trying to bring his friend back.

"Oscar!" Vivienne's voice strained as she reached a hand out to stop his movements. "What are you doing?"

"Saving Brutus," he grunted, trying to tug his arm free.

"Darling, it's too late. He's too far gone."

"No," he screamed at her, pushing her away and inching closer to his furry friend. "I don't believe it. I can bring him back."

"With your blood?" Gareth asked incredulously.

"Yes," he hissed. Why was it so difficult for them to understand? Gareth was the one who said Brutus reminded him of an angry vampire the day they met him. Why couldn't Brutus become a vampire then?

"My dear…" Vivienne's voice was soft and gentle, taking his hand away once again. "You know as well as I do, it's not going to work."

Oscar's shoulders slumped in defeat. He'd let his little buddy down. "But… if I… just tried…"

"I know," she said in a soothing tone, pulling him to her chest. "I feel the same."

Taste of Revenge

Oscar Van Wilden had not shed a tear since Delizera's death. But his eyes stung, and water blurred his vision. His body shuddered with his grief as Vivienne's arms tightened, burying her head into the crook of his neck.

A roar erupted from his mouth before he could control himself. Losing the campaign, one daughter imprisoned for trying to kill his wife, another daughter abducted, and now his dog was dead. He unwrapped Vivienne's arms from around him and charged inside the house, not caring if he ripped the heavy oak door off its hinges.

Concern flooded the bond from his wife. "Oscar?"

He ignored her, picked up his favorite armchair in both hands before tearing the piece of furniture in half. He flung the broken pieces away from him, knocking over his liquor table. Shards of glass and amber liquid splashed everywhere, seeping into the floorboards and rugs.

"Oscar Van Wilden, you will cease destroying our home this instant," Vivienne yelled, her icy-blue eyes on fire as she stood with her hands on her hips.

Gareth and Alastor stood next to her, their eyes wide, both of their mouths gaping open.

Once again, he ignored her, the rage coursing through his body drowning out every coherent thought. He stormed out of the house.

"We better follow him." Vivienne's voice carried out to him as he ran straight for the town lair location.

He didn't care if their base of operations wasn't there anymore. Any vampires in his path would be shredded—the body parts left too small for them ever to merge back together and regenerate, their ashes scattering on the wind choking everyone around them.

They would regret killing his fucking dog.

Oscar didn't know which way he was running, and he didn't care. His grief and rage blinded him to all else but the thoughts of Brutus' forlorn body.

He felt them before he heard them, cawing and laughing amongst themselves. A group of four young males.

"Yow, yow, yowl," one howled toward the night sky.

"Yeah, did you see how it squirmed. Stupid dog."

Oscar's teeth grated against each other and heat crept up his neck. They'd witnessed Brutus' demise.

He leaped out of the shadows roaring like a monster.

"Run!" one screamed as they hightailed it away.

Taste of Revenge

Pathetic. Oscar caught the one who howled by his collar, grasping him by the neck with his other hand. "Where's your leader?"

The vampire rasped and clawed at Oscar's hand.

"Fine. Don't talk, but *you will* take me with you. First, your friends." Oscar dragged the vampire alongside, gurgling noises erupting as his grip tightened.

They killed his fucking dog.

He followed the others who were leading him to the abandoned town lair.

How ironic.

These vampires were either dumb or weren't trained to know what to do. They were quick, reaching the house well before him, but nothing beats the wrath of a Primus finding his beloved puppy dead.

When he caught up to them a mere minute later, he threw their comrade into them like a bowling ball, knocking them down like pins resulting in stunned expressions.

His lips pulled back, baring his fangs as his hand touched the stakes at his waist.

Oscar stood over them. "Like to take joy in watching innocent animals die, do you?" He lunged for all four of them and seized the vampire he had thrown, whose olive eyes darted around the room as the others were trying to shove him off of them. Oscar wanted to rip the vampire's torso apart but refrained from doing so in case the body wouldn't burn. He settled with slamming the body down on his knee, severing the kid's spine, then he pulled out a stake and jammed it into his lifeless chest.

"Dude." One of the other vampires—a preppy looking kid, with sandy hair styled into a quiff, now untangled from the others—put up his palms and shuffled backward.

Oscar grunted and lit the stake in the vampire he held, then tossed the burning vampire aside. The flames licked his skin, but the burns would heal. That pain was nothing compared to the hurt he was experiencing from seeing Brutus' dead body.

He leaped forward, fisting the other vampire's white t-shirt, hauling him up close. The vampire's eyes, a dark tawny color, widened before Oscar's other hand whipped forward ramming a stake into his torso, piercing the lungs and muscles to reach the heart. With his hand inside the vampire's chest, Oscar realized his grave mistake. By plunging the stake into the heart through the inside of the body, the stake would unlikely set alight. *Bollocks.* He flung the body away from him, his hand now coated in blood, and he grabbed another stake. He crouched down and stabbed the wooden weapon into the front of the chest this time.

He looked up to see another vampire scrambling in the dirt to get away from him. Oscar stood and lunged for him. The vampire's black eyes widened, his beige skin took on a pallid color. He turned, running two steps before Oscar grabbed his long black hair tied at the nape of his neck. The vampire's back arched, and he howled. The sound was familiar. *This was the one who had howled before. How ironic he was howling now like Brutus inevitably had.* Oscar's other hand flipped a stake around and rammed it into the vampire's temple.

One vampire left. *This must have been the one who'd made fun of Brutus.* His lips and chin trembled, making his black beard bobble up and down. Didn't any of these vampires shave when they were human? Oscar's roar echoed around the empty neighborhood as he leaped onto the vampire still lying on the ground from when his comrade had knocked him over. He'd watched the whole scene, mouth agape, like a fish.

Oscar landed on his body. Straddling the kid, he grasped the vampire's head, his black hair shaved close to his scalp. The vampire hollered, his caramel face twisting as Oscar ripped his head apart like a stale loaf of bread. Blood, skin, and skull shards flew everywhere, and the brain plopped out onto the ground. *Shit.* The whole body had to be together to burn.

He lifted himself off the dead vampire and went to retrieve the organ, placing it back inside the jagged, fragmented skull as best as he could. He plunged a stake into his heart, lighting the ends quickly while holding the brain inside the skull.

Once the body was aflame, he let go of the head and turned to the others. The vampire with a stake in his head was beginning to revive. The stake was slowing coming out of his skull.

"Stay fucking dead," Oscar growled, taking another stake out of his holster and sinking it into the vampire's chest. The body twitched, and the olive eyes were lifeless once more.

He lit the end of the stake and turned to the other with the two stakes in his body and set the protruding stake on fire.

Oscar stood looking around him at the burning bodies, his chest heaving. Vivienne, Gareth, and Alastor approached.

"Did you question them first for the whereabouts of Morgana?" Vivienne asked, watching the flames burn out, the bodies combusting into ash.

"I had meant to." He howled at his stupidity. *He was a Council Elder after all.* He shouldn't have let his emotions rule him. He turned toward the house and began smashing his fists into the walls as chunks of mortar and bricks went flying.

"Jaysus," Alastor cursed.

"Fuck," Gareth exclaimed.

"Oscar, stop this nonsense at once," Vivienne snapped.

"Aye, we'll stop him, Mrs. V."

"Don't hurt yourselves in the process."

A hand clamped down on his shoulder, stilling his vandalism. He turned his head to see Gareth's eyes full of sympathy. "I feel like doing the same thing. But you have to be the level-headed one here. Without Morgana to boss us around, we've only got you to keep old Irish and me in line."

"And you, too, Mrs. V," he said hastily when she opened her mouth to protest.

"We need the stern Oscar Van Wilden to stare us down and put us in our place. We need you to be the Elder we've come to know and respect. Our coven…" he waved a hand at the other two, "…needs our leader. And she's being held somewhere."

Oscar grunted, but his lips twitched.

Gareth grinned. "So, you need to be our leader. Teach us two knuckleheads…" he motioned to Alastor, "… strategies and scouting techniques to find Morgana."

"Aye, I miss Brutus, too." Alastor stepped up. "What they did was feckin' wrong. And the bastards will pay, don't ye worry about that. But we need ye." Alastor gazed at him as he spoke.

Oscar's shoulders slumped. He pulled his hands away from the destruction. "Thank you. You're right. I wasn't myself. In fact, I don't know if I've been myself for quite a while. But what I do know is I'm sorry for my behavior. Now and recently. I shouldn't have kept Mariza's imprisonment from all of you."

Alastor nodded.

"Good. Then let's get back to the house. We'll bury Brutus in the morning."

In keeping with the town's theme, in their backyard grew an old oak on the border of the forest.

"I suppose it is only fitting I bury him under this tree, considering we adopted him here." Oscar drove the shovel into the mound of dirt he'd created.

A sniffle came from Vivienne. Immense sadness filled their bond from both their ends.

Gareth dipped his head, staring at the small grave Oscar had dug for Brutus. "Morgana will be devastated when she hears about this."

Ava nodded, holding on to Alastor's hand. Tears trickled down her cheek.

"He was only in our lives for a short time, but he was family." Oscar placed Brutus' still body into the ground. "Even though you were not a Primus, may you return to bone and ash. May you take with you our love to wherever it is that you will find peace."

Oscar squatted and placed a handful of dirt on top of Brutus. "Farewell, my friend."

Vivienne walked up next and threw her handful gracefully over his forlorn body. "Mommy will miss you, running after you when you knocked breakables over and even your loud barking."

Gareth, Alastor, and Ava also threw their handfuls of dirt into the grave.

"Do you want us to fill it in for you?" Gareth asked Oscar.

"No. I think I should do this myself."

"Okay." Gareth patted his shoulder.

"I'm staying to help." Vivienne lifted her chin. Oscar nodded. He felt the determination from her. He wasn't going to argue with her. Not over this.

"I'm going to take Ava back to her place, and then I'll be back," Alastor told them.

"I'm sorry for your loss," Ava said to Oscar and Vivienne.

"Aye, as am I."

Oscar gave them a grim look. "Thank you both. Keep yourselves safe on the way. Who knows who else they'll try to target next."

CHAPTER 28

Rivulets of blood trickled down her arms and legs.
The smell assaulting her senses.
Even though it was her blood, her body still craved it.
Dying and in need of blood to sustain her.
To replenish all that she had lost.
All that blood at her feet, and she couldn't drink a single drop.

Morgana opened her eyes to see Ragnorok standing there, leering as he held up another goblet full of her blood. "My revenge is going to taste oh so sweet. Have I told you I've spent all this time discovering everything I could about you, your parents, and The Council. All for this moment. My turn to eliminate you all."

Taste of Revenge

Ragnorok sipped her blood, making an appreciative groan. "You taste so good... delicate and smooth like liquid velvet coating my tongue."

Morgana ground her teeth, pushing against the chains. "I'm going to rip out your heart," she vowed. She was going to make sure she inflicted as much pain and agony on him as he was doing to her. *How dare he taunt her like this!?* Drinking her blood like it was a goddamn wine tasting. Never again was she going to get herself into a position to be used as a blood bag. After this, no one was going to drink her blood ever again.

And to add to the humiliation, they'd cut her leather pants up to her inner thighs to allow more blood to drain. The metal burned into her skin when she moved.

"Yes, that's it, get your heart rate up. It'll pump more blood out of your body."

Morgana's head slumped forward. He was right, and it was making her woozy as the blood drained out.

"I'm going to kill you," she hissed through clenched teeth.

"We'll see." He sipped from his goblet before handing the goblet over to a nearby vampire, whose face she couldn't see. He handed Ragnorok a handkerchief from his shirt pocket. The Forest Clan leader wiped the blood from his mouth. "Oh, and speaking of eliminating you all, your little family *pet* is already dead."

Morgana's eyes widened. Her heart ached as she strained against the chains. Her eyes squeezed shut. "You didn't!"

"Oh, but I did. Reports are coming in that your father trashed our old town lair in his wrath rampage."

"You're pathetic, killing weak innocents!" Tears stung her eyes. Morgana wasn't much of a crier but hearing her beloved family pet had been killed warranted them in this case.

Ragnorok grasped her chin, squeezing her cheeks, "No. You're pathetically weak."

She tried to wrench her face free but failed. "It's because of vampires like you that I have to do my job."

"And it's vampires, or in your case, half-vampires, like you that I have to do my job cleansing the human race of disgusting weaklings. You and your followers are killing vampires just for living like vampires were intended. *You* are the monsters."

Morgana pushed against the chains once more. "You killed a dog, a sweet, innocent, beautiful dog. There's no honor in that. And *you will* pay the price for *all* of your crimes."

"You killed *her*," Ragnorok screamed, inches from her face. "She was *my family,* and *you* killed her."

"Who?" Morgana's eyes narrowed before realization hit her. "Angelique?"

Ragnorok pulled his face back, astonished. "So, *now* you remember?"

"Oh, I remember her well. How she was getting fucked while her entire clan was being eradicated," she spat.

"You lie. All she ever did was what was best for us."

"She wiped out the few remaining humans left in the old country. She took it too far."

"Says who? A bunch of ancient vampires who were born instead of turned? How is that *just?* How is that *fair?*"

"Wiping out humans isn't doing the vampire race any favors. They're our food source. We do it for the good of the vampire society."

"No, you do it for your pumped-up egos that try to tell others what to do. How to feed."

"This type of feeding..." she looked down at the blood pooling around her feet and up toward the other girls chained in a similar fashion, "... is barbaric."

Ragnorok waved his arms around. "No, this way it feeds my whole clan, not just myself. This is smart." He tapped his temple.

"No, it's —"

"Argh!" Ragnorok grabbed his face. "Will someone shut her up!"

"Will do, boss." A gangly vampire reached up with the silver knife and before she could protest, sliced into Morgana's throat.

Blood spilled out of her mouth, and she glared with as much hatred as she could at Ragnorok before her head slumped forward and darkness took over once again.

CHAPTER 29

Morgana awoke to spots of searing pain starting from her hips and spreading across her abdomen. She moved her head down as far as she could to see several stakes whittled from different scented woods, protruding from her body.

"Ah, good, you're awake." Ragnorok chatted to her like this was casual banter. "You can tell me which one is hurting you the most."

The fucker smiled at her. If her mouth weren't so dry from dehydration, she would have spat at him. All she could manage was a venomous glare.

"Now, now, don't be like that. I just want you to tell me whether it's painful, deadly, or nothing?"

"Like hell, I will," she gritted.

"Tsk. Tsk. You're just prolonging the agony. Tell me, and I'll stop."

"No."

Ragnorok grasped her face in his hand, squeezing hard. She struggled to break free. But too much of her strength had already leeched out of her.

Bloody hell, this silver was doing a real number on her.

"Tell me which one kills them!"

She stared at him defiantly. No matter how much torture and pain Ragnorok inflicted on her, she would never tell him. It had been honed into her how important it was to keep this secret.

Hell, she would have never told Gareth and Alastor if it hadn't been a matter of life or death. But now it wasn't just her life. It was everyone she knew and had grown up with—her father, her brothers, other agents, and the Council Elders, themselves.

As much as she didn't want to die, sacrificing her life to take the secret of killing a Primus to the grave would be the right thing to do.

So, she remained silent.

She could work through the pain. She'd escape. She'd already done it once. She could do it again because she couldn't die anyway. Unless she told Ragnorok how, and there was no way she was going to break and tell him.

At least she knew Mariza hadn't completely betrayed them. Her sister never told the Forest Clan leader about hawthorn.

Taste of Revenge

"Fine, we'll keep going! More!" he snapped, continuing his torture of her by repeatedly stabbing her chest, arms, and thighs. She clenched her teeth and bared it, her eyes stung with tears, leaking of their own accord. Next time she staked a vampire—Ragnorok being the exception—she was going to do it as quick and pain-free as possible. This torture was agony.

"Now, my dear, this is the final one," Ragnorok spoke into her ear. Her vision was becoming blurry again. She could barely lift her head to face him.

"I think I have saved the best for last. This *has* to be the right one." He pulled the tip of the stake across the parts of skin that remained on her stomach. Morgana tried not to wince at the burn following the stake's path. But from the pain inflicted on her, and the instinct to shy away from the smell, it was hawthorn, the only wood able to kill a Primus and their children.

"You still aren't showing any signs of pain," Ragnorok admired. "But I can see the effect the hawthorn is having on your skin. It's reddening around the cut I made." Ragnorok held out the stake to his second-in-command. "It's this one. Go and put it somewhere safe until we need it. Gather up the others. We have a trip to make."

"No." Morgana's voice was ragged as she tried to stay conscious, but the hawthorn was seeping into her blood. Bleary-eyed, she slumped forward, welcoming the reprieve from the pain with the darkness.

After a long and emotional day with Brutus' funeral, Ava readied herself for bed. As she was sliding under the covers, her open laptop screen lit up, beeping at her from its position where she'd moved it to on her bedside table. Her brow furrowed. She groaned while sitting back up to see what the alert was about.

Her father had sent her an email.

> Hey, sweetheart,
> The police think they have a new lead on the missing person case. They think they are being taken to the old abandoned estate set to be redeveloped in the next few weeks. We'll investigate further in the morning.
> Dad.

Ava groaned. That was the location of the abandoned Forest Clan town lair. If her father or the police went there, they would surely know something not 'normal' was going on in the town. And that would be the last thing any of them wanted.

Taste of Revenge

They couldn't risk it.

She swung her legs over the edge of the bed, weighing up her options. She could call the Van Wildens and let them know her father and the sheriff were going to investigate the old town lair. Or she could go herself and cover up anything out of the ordinary. Ava decided to go with option two. The Van Wildens were too occupied with searching for Morgana. They wouldn't want to be bothered by something like this. This was something Ava could do *for* them.

Even though Oscar had said to remain in the safety of her apartment, she shrugged it off and walked over to her wardrobe to change into black leggings and a sweater. She tied her blonde hair back into a low bun at the nape of her neck and placed a black woolen slouchy beanie on top. She looked at herself in the mirror. *She would have looked cooler if it were a beret.*

She shook her head and grabbed her runners from the bottom of the closet. Entering the living room, she grabbed her trusty notepad and pen, slipping them into the sweater pocket. *You never knew when you'd need to write something down.* Then she grabbed her phone and keys.

She parked her car in an alley a block away from the old town lair. She couldn't run all over the place like the others. She killed the engine and climbed out.

She breathed deeply. *I'm going to be fine.* The arrival of the Van Wildens had brought with them a wealth of knowledge, one being wolfsbane, a sort of apotropaic—a dangerous substance to human-turned vampires. When the young women started being taken Morgana has supplied her with the apotropaic. Much to Alastor's chagrin. Before Ava had left the house, she had mixed it in with her strawberry lotion and slathered it on her skin. That way she might be able to get away.

Besides, she was too old for them to take her anyway. The Forest Clan had been kidnapping teenagers and college-age humans. And there shouldn't be any vampires around here anyway. Between the Forest Clan abandoning this lair and Oscar's rampage after finding Brutus' dead body, the town had been void of vampires for the last two nights.

She should be safe.

Ragnorok stood back, admiring the halfling's slumped form. Truly it was a work of art. The silver twisted around her body contrasting against the rivers of red trickling down her limbs and torso. Some had even matted in her dark hair.

Truly magnificent.

"My Lord," Cedric spoke behind him.

A muscle in his cheek twitched. "What now?" How dare he be interrupted his moment of satisfaction. He turned around to face his new second-in-command. Svetlana would have left him be before coming to address him.

Cedric held that rectangular device in his hand. "Forgive me…"

Good, he was learning.

"… but you wanted to know of the Irish Daywalker's mate's movements at all times."

"And?"

"She's at the old lair location. And she's alone."

Stupid girl. But another win for them.

Ragnorok smiled. "I think I'll also attend this rather special extraction."

CHAPTER 30

Ava tiptoed her way over to the lair using the torch app on her phone.

She had never really been out here with the others, so the sight of the demolished house was shocking to take in. Large chunks of brick and mortar lay scattered everywhere, leaving large gaping holes in the walls of the house. If she hadn't been receiving regular updates and knew it was Oscar who had caused the destruction, she would have thought the place had been hit with a wrecking ball. *Well, this would save the demolishers some effort and time.*

Sometimes she wondered, despite what she'd said to Alastor the other night, what it would be like to have a vampire's strength and speed. She worked out at the gym regularly, so she was quite fit, but the thought of all that power still intrigued her.

Taste of Revenge

Ava stilled. She groaned inward at her stupidity. She was human and alone investigating the abandoned town lair in the middle of the night. It was like one of the scary movies she made Alastor watch so she could gauge his reaction as fact or fiction. Even though she couldn't sense or hear the vampires as the others could, she'd been around them long enough to know when they were approaching her. Maybe it was deeply instinctual—prey sensing the danger of a predator nearby.

And like life imitating art, they crept out of the shadows stalking toward her, just like how the movies portrayed them as monsters of the night. Their leader, with his dead gray eyes, was the most evil-looking of them all.

Ragnorok smiled as he stepped toward her. "Well, this is another lucky break for me. I was wondering when I'd be able to get my hands on you."

"Why, what do you want with me?" she stammered, taking small steps back.

"Oh, little human, I've been watching you for a while now."

She quickly turned and ran knowing they would catch her. But she wasn't going to make it easy for them. She pulled out her phone and dialed Alastor.

"Ava, love?" That rich Irish accent she loved so much coming from the other end.

"Alastor," she huffed into the phone, snarls behind her made her turn her head. They were almost upon her. "They're coming for me."

The line went dead. It took Alastor a second for his brain to register what was occurring. "Aye, love?" he shouted into the phone, his stomach tightening. The others turned to look at him, questions in their eyes.

"Jaysus feckin' Christ. The bastards are takin' Ava!" he roared, springing from his chair and racing toward the front door.

"Alastor, stop!" Oscar commanded. Alastor skidded across the wooden floors trying to gain traction. No matter how determined he was to save Ava, it was nigh impossible to ignore the authority in the voice of the Elder.

"Arm yourself before you charge off recklessly."

Alastor turned and arched an eyebrow at Oscar.

"Do as I say and not what I did," Oscar grumbled standing up. "And we're coming with you. Ava is part of this coven. I won't let her be taken, too."

Alastor's face softened.

"Yes." Vivienne stood. "Let's stop him from taking another of my family members."

Alastor's chin dipped to his chest. "Aye, thank ye both."

Taste of Revenge

Gareth clapped a hand on his shoulder. "We're each other's coven, remember? Where you go, I go."

Vivienne placed her hand on Alastor's other shoulder. "All of us."

Alastor nodded. His eyes itched, and he rubbed at them. Vivienne leaned closer to him, dropping her voice, "That'll be your body trying to shed a tear." She squeezed his shoulder, giving him a sympathetic smile.

"It bloody hurts."

"I know." Her eyes also looked red.

"If you two are done, can we go rescue my friend now? At least we can stop them this time." Gareth looked away quickly, but Alastor saw his best friend's eyes had also become red.

He smiled, grateful for each of them in his life and what they were willing to do for his girlfriend. "Aye, let's go get me girl."

CHAPTER 31

Alastor and the others headed toward Ava's apartment to search for clues as to where she may have gone.

Her laptop was open on her bed, and the email from her father was still on the screen. Alastor flipped it around to read it.

"Feckin' hell." Alastor rubbed his face, and Vivienne gasped reading the screen over his shoulder.

"Where did she go?" Gareth asked.

"She feckin' went to the old town lair."

Oscar closed his eyes. "This is indeed not good news. Not good news at all."

"We feckin' need to leave and get over there now!"

Taste of Revenge

They ran toward the town lair site.

Alastor couldn't see Ava anywhere, but there was an abundance of vampires inside the ruins. He rushed forward and ran headlong into a group of vampires emerging who looked startled to see them.

Alastor swung his fist connecting to the closest vampire's nose, the long sandy-haired youth's head snapped back, and blood smeared across his face. Alastor grabbed a stake and stabbed the vampire before he could retaliate. He stepped over the fallen vampire, moving onto the next. He could see Gareth out of the corner of his eye, jumping from foot to foot like a boxer before striking. Oscar was on the other side of him, gripping the back of a vampire's neck, lifting him into the air before slamming him into the ground and staking him there.

Vivienne was following behind them and lighting the stakes causing each one to combust into ash. "Boys, make sure you stake then set them on fire." She shook her head.

Alastor smiled at the sight of his coven having his back. There must have been something scary about his smile as the vampire in front of him put up his hand and looked around wildly, backing away. Alastor's grin grew wider as he drew a stake from his holster advancing toward him. "Where's me girl?"

The vampire pointed behind his finger to a spot behind Alastor.

"I'd cease your activities if I were you." The cold voice and familiar presence of Ragnorok turned their attention away from the skirmish.

He stood with his arm wrapped around a whimpering blonde's torso. His fangs hovering inches from her collarbone, a painful grimace on his face. The faint whiff of artificial strawberries mixed with wolfsbane would explain why.

"Ava!" he cried, racing toward them.

"Uh ah uh," Ragnorok taunted, cocking a finger at him.

Stakes sailed past him, embedding themselves into Alastor's shoulders, chest, and stomach, missing his heart by a mere inch. He grunted, his movements sluggish as he tried to walk toward his love, his arm stretched out to her.

"Nice touch, isn't it? I picked that up from watching the half-breed."

"Alastor!" Both Vivienne and Gareth shouted out at the same time. Screams rent the air as more stakes flew around him, hitting his friends.

Oscar flew past him, stakes sticking out of him like a pin cushion. "Let her go," he roared.

"Give her back," Alastor cried, leaning toward them.

Ragnorok tilted his head. "Why do you even care? She's only human."

"Not to us, she isn't," Oscar growled. Ava let out a tearful sob at his words, a tear trickled out of her left eye. The Primus was but a foot away from reaching Ava.

Ragnorok just smiled as another stake flew forward.

Alastor slumped forward on his knees, still reaching out for Ava as he caught the scent of a single stake sailing toward Oscar.

The Elder grunted, stopping him in his tracks as it pierced his gut.

Hawthorn.

Shit, *they knew.*

"Bring the others," Ragnorok told them. "I'll be waiting."

Alastor looked up, his vision blurring as Ragnorok turned away with Ava, then everything went dark.

Alastor bolted upright, "Ava!"

Looking around, he was in the guestroom of the Van Wilden's place. Vivienne was perched on the side of the bed.

"Where is she?" He tore the bed covers off his body. Vivienne placed a hand on his shoulder, stilling his movements.

"Most likely the same place they have Morgana."

"We need to find them."

"And we will, Alastor. But you need to build your strength back up. You were one stake away from being pierced in the heart. You and Oscar were riddled with them. Even Gareth copped a few. It took all my strength to go back and forth carrying you all back to the house."

"Thanks," he mumbled.

Vivienne gave him a small smile and passed him a large stein of blood. "Drink this up, and we'll make plans to find them."

"Aye." Alastor took the blood and swallowed a large mouthful. "Where's the boy?"

"Still recovering."

"And how's Mr. V? That last stake missed his heart, but I was sure it was hawthorn."

"It was, but he has recovered. He heals faster than the rest of us, being so old."

Despite the dire situation, Alastor gave a small chuckle.

"It only kills them when it's through the heart. He was just poisoned."

"Where's he now?"

"Giving Ohana's dummy a workout."

Alastor winced. "That poor training dummy ain't going to last much longer at this rate." It wasn't too long ago he was taking his anger about Mariza out on that dummy.

Vivienne laughed quietly. "If you're feeling better, then please go check on Gareth. I'm going to stop Oscar and get him to drink something."

"Aye, that I can do."

"We'll get her back, Alastor," Vivienne said fiercely, "Both of them. Alive."

"Aye."

Vivienne gave him a small nod before leaving the room.

Alastor finished the rest of his blood before setting the glass down on the bedside table. His strength was returning. Good. He swung his legs over to the side of the bed, his head snapping up when he heard groans of agony coming from Morgana's bedroom.

Gareth.

CHAPTER 32

Gareth was stumbling around in the dark calling out for her.

"I'm here, Gareth." Her voice floated over to him.

"Where?"

"Here."

"But I can't see you."

Morgana materialized in front of his face, her body fuzzy around the edges like she was a ghost.

"I'm here," she said, tapping on his heart. "Right where I've always been." Her face hovered closer. "Feel where I am."

His body began writhing with pain. It was like he was on fire with blood pouring out of his skin.

In the distance, he heard a male voice calling out to him.

"Morgana," he cried.

"That's where I am, Gareth. Follow the pain."

Morgana disappeared, but her voice remained. "Come find me where the wild rose stood."

Morgana lifted her head with as much strength as she could muster. All the Forest vampires were gone, except for a single vampire standing before her, the edges around him looked blurry.

"Gareth?"

"I'm here, my love. Hang in there." He held her head in his hands, but his touch didn't feel solid. "Remember to keep the bond open. I'm coming for you."

Then he faded into the air, and Morgana slumped forward.

There was no one there.

No one was coming for her.

Once again, Morgana was on her own.

Gareth's shoulders were being shaken, and he bolted upright almost headbutting Alastor who was kneeling on the bed, his hands gripping Gareth's shoulders.

"Bloody hell. Ye scared the fuckin' shit out of me," Alastor shouted.

"Morgana," Gareth rasped, looking wildly at his best friend. He'd been wrong. He'd been trying to find her through the bond by feeling her love, happier emotions, even anger. He had never considered feeling for her pain. Whatever Ragnorok was doing to her, she was in a lot of pain. He concentrated on finding her. And once again, his body convulsed with the same pain that radiated throughout her body. She was screaming in agony. Gareth was screaming.

The door flew open, and Oscar strode in with Vivienne at his heels.

"He just keeps convulsing," he could hear Alastor saying.

Gareth could feel Morgana's pain like her flesh was being torn apart. This one burned through to her bones. He'd felt something similar before. He just couldn't quite place where.

"Gareth." Oscar stood over him, holding his body still.

"What's going on?" Vivienne sounded concerned.

"Morgana." The cry ripped from his mouth, and his body flopped back onto the mattress.

"Jaysus Christ."

Gareth tried to sit up with Alastor's help. He looked wildly around at them. "I know where they are."

Taste of Revenge

Moments later, Gareth sat at the kitchen island, a large glass of blood in his hands. Ironically, this is where he and Morgana had first discovered they had a bond. Now he was using it to find her.

"He's torturing her," Gareth whispered. "I could feel her pain."

Vivienne gasped, her hand going to her chest.

"Tell me where they are, son?" Oscar placed his hand on his shoulder.

"I kept trying to feel her good feelings," Gareth mumbled. "But she told me to feel for her pain instead. She said to find them where the wild roses stood." He looked up meeting Vivienne's eyes—a much lighter shade of blue than his, but now wide with recognition.

They all knew the spot—where Mariza had taken Vivienne to fight her to the death. Where Alastor had thought he'd killed Mariza.

"Feckin' hell," the Irish vampire muttered.

Oscar withdrew his hand and sat back on a vacant stool, looking stumped. "Back to where the cage of wild rose was?"

"Yes."

Oscar pulled out his phone, finger swiping over the screen. "I'm calling for backup."

"Who?" Vivienne asked, clutching at the front of her shirt.

Oscar held up his hand, and they heard a deep male voice answer. "Pops?"

"Hello, son."

CHAPTER 33

Gareth paced up and down the living room. "Why can't we go get them? We know where the girls are? What are we standing around here for?"

"Patience, Gareth. We can't just go in there without a strategy. We need to plan our assault."

"I'll say." The deep voice made Gareth's head snap around to see two tall vampires enter the living room. They must have been drenched in wolfsbane for him not to have sensed them.

Gareth stood tall at six feet, but these two looked like giants.

The one on the left look liked a younger version of Oscar. The Council Elder was ageless, but he still had an air radiating about him that he was indeed old. He stood a few inches taller than Gareth. He'd thought he'd seen him somewhere before.

The one on the right was massive, at least a foot taller than the other at seven feet. Gareth had broad shoulders, but this guy was built like a professional wrestler—he had arms and legs the size of tree trunks. His dark hair was shaved close to his scalp. But what gave away they were Morgana's brothers were their eyes.

The Van Wilden eyes—dark, deep depths of chocolate brown.

Their bronze skin tones were a darker shade than Morgana's, though.

"Sons." Oscar stood to greet them, embracing them both.

"Father," the one on the left said.

"Pops!" grinned the wrestler.

Oscar wasn't short either, but he was dwarfed by his two sons. They must have gotten their height from their mother.

"Jonas, Hector." Vivienne also stood sniffing.

Gareth suddenly remembered where he'd seen the shorter one, at the mention of his name. Morgana had been FaceTiming her brother, Jonas, when they'd received their punishment, him for killing Randalf and Morgana for going off on her own without The Council's permission.

"We're here to help rescue Morgana, Vivienne," Jonas said quietly.

Vivienne broke into sobs and rushed over, hugging them both at the same time.

Jonas and Hector shared a look, patting her awkwardly on the back.

Gareth didn't know what the look was about, but he would ask about it later.

Right now, he was intrigued by Morgana's brothers.

Were they friend or foe?

He stood, feeling Alastor flanking him.

"Ah, yes, sons, I'd like you to meet Morgana's mate, Gareth, and another member of our coven, his friend, Alastor."

"I've heard great things about you both." Jonas smiled, holding out his hand.

Gareth took his outstretched hand, shaking it, trying not to grimace from his strength. Jonas withdrew his hand, placing his palms up. "Sorry, wasn't trying to intimidate you. I forgot you're human-turned."

"Yeah, especially after killing off old Randy." Hector's voice boomed as he slapped him heartily on the back, making Gareth jerk forward. Hector leaned over, grasping his arm and helping him back up. "Sorry, bro." He turned to Alastor. "And you, Irish, taking down our sis."

"Aye." Alastor watching them closely, his shoulders tensed.

Jonas and Hector exchanged a look before bursting out laughing. "Come here, bro." Hector engulfed Alastor into a bone-crushing hug. He placed Alastor back down on the floor. "Don't feel so bad, Riza had it coming. Someone was bound to stake her eventually." Oscar cleared his throat. "What, Pops? It's true. I'm glad you ended up switching the stakes around. She can be a pain, but she's still my sister." He turned back to Alastor. "But you did good, Irish, you did good," he continued, ruffling Alastor's copper locks.

Jonas gave him a sympathetic smile before holding his hand out to him. "I'm not as much of a hugger as my brother."

Alastor grinned and shook Jonas' hand. "Aye, nice to meet ye."

Jonas looked toward Vivienne. "They've both been trained well."

Vivienne grinned, holding her chin high with a gleam in her eye as she pulled her two stepsons into another hug. They exchanged another look between them before relaxing into her hold.

"How is Mariza?" Oscar asked quietly when they pulled back from her.

"She's settling in there now," Jonas replied. "First week she screamed like a banshee and kept throwing herself up against the bars."

"I hope she's not too bored in there."

"We give her books to read and movies to watch. I visit her once a week to keep her updated on the outside world."

"Good, good." Oscar looked down at the glass of whiskey in his hands. "Once this mission is over, I'd like to go see her."

Taste of Revenge

Jonas squeezed his father's shoulder. "I'm sure she'd like that very much."

Oscar nodded.

Throughout their conversation, Gareth glanced at Alastor and Vivienne, gauging their reactions. His best friend's eyes were focused on the wall, his jaw clenched. He was hoping his evil creator of a bitch was suffering. Vivienne had her lemon-sucking face again.

When the conversation ended, her face brightened and flashed a smile around, but it was her campaign-trail smile.

But you also couldn't mistake the sadness in Oscar's voice when he spoke of his other daughter. Now was not a time to rehash their issues and hatred toward Mariza.

And while it was nice to meet Morgana's brothers, and to see them resolving some sort of family issue between them and Vivienne, this was wasting time. "Look, I hate to break up this family reunion, but can't we do this after rescuing Morgana?"

Jonas nodded. "Yes. We scouted out the scene before we got here."

"Why didn't you get her, then?" Gareth thundered.

"Because they have a fucking army, dude." Hector stood with his arms crossed over his chest.

"An army?" Oscar wiped his brow. "How many?"

"About three hundred."

Gareth quickly did the math. They were going to be outnumbered forty to one. "We can take them." He stood tall, his chest out, chin lifted.

Hector chuckled. "I like your attitude. We're good, but we're not *that* good."

"I looked up Ragnorok's creator, Angelique." Jonas was looking down at his smartphone. "She was one of Dieter Dovkosky's first creations."

Oscar sighed heavily.

Gareth tossed the name Dovkosky around in his brain. Why did it sound so familiar? Then it hit him. "Dovkosky. They were the ones who started the war?"

All three Van Wilden men turned to him with incredulous stares.

"How do you know that?" Oscar asked.

Gareth shrugged. "Randalf told me. He was trying to prove I wasn't worthy of being an agent."

"Good thing you offed the arrogant bastard, then," Hector said.

"Shit." Oscar rubbed his face. Now everyone turned to look at him with incredulous faces. Oscar rarely swore. "They're trying to recreate the war."

"That would explain why Angelique created a vampire called Ragnorok," said Jonas.

"They are trying to take down The Council." Oscar grimaced. "We need the others."

"Yeah, but wouldn't that be playing right into this guy's hand bringing them all out here?"

Hector nodded.

"My sons, who is it that won the war the first time?"

"We did," they both answered.

"And we shall win again. No one takes my daughter, one of my coven members, kills my dog, and lives to see the day end."

"You had a dog?" Hector asked incredulously. "How come we didn't get to have a dog growing up?"

"If I recall correctly, our village didn't have the necessary means to raise pets," Jonas said dryly.

"We should gather up the other Primus and ask them to come to our aid." Oscar rose from his chair.

The doorbell rang, causing Oscar to raise an eyebrow.

Gareth realized he missed the sounds of Brutus' bark and seeing him scramble over his large puppy feet to get to the door. Even Vivienne's eyes were red and scratchy as she looked at his bed in the corner.

Jonas rubbed the back of his neck. "Well, I was hoping you'd feel that way, Father, because I've already invited them."

CHAPTER 34

In the early hours of the morning, Morgana's mind was still alert but trapped in her weakened body like a painful and bullet-ridden fleshy prison.

How long had she been like this? Hours? Days? Had it reached a week yet? She was so tired. All she wanted to do was crawl into bed and pull the covers over her head, her body ached from being upright for so long. But what would they do to her if she slept? From her slumped position, her head dangled at a precarious angle, her eyes roved over her body, and the rivers of blood were still trickling down her limbs.

Really, there wasn't much more they could do to her.

Physically.

Psychologically, they had other plans.

A strange scent lifted Morgana's head.

She knew that smell.

Sweet artificial strawberries.

No. No. No. It felt like someone had taken hold of her heart and crushed it in their hands as she watched two vampires drag Ava's lifeless body between them and strap her to the pole adjacent to hers.

Morgana struggled against the chains, the silver digging into her burned flesh further, trying to get to her.

She could handle the pain, the poisoning, the torture, and the taunts. Sure, she outwardly put on a tough bravado. But on the inside, seeing her friend in the same position as her, helpless to do anything about it, *that* nearly broke her.

"Morgana," Ava whispered.

Morgana's head remained slumped forward.

"Listen to me, Morgana."

Morgana could barely lift her head. They had won.

"Stay strong. They're coming for us."

Morgana's eyes shifted to look at her friend. "No. No one is coming for me."

"Yes, they are," Ava hissed. "Listen…"

Ava's cry brought her out of her stupor.

Ragnorok had her friend by the hair, forcing her chin up to face him.

"You know, you really *should* listen to your friend here. Of course, they're coming to rescue you. This whole ruse is designed for them to come here. And die." He leaned closer to Ava. "You know you have quite the pretty mouth." His lips hovered over hers as Ava squirmed.

"Don't you dare touch her," Morgana gritted.

Ragnorok sighed, leaning back. "But I've had enough of blonde lovers. You know the last blonde I fucked was your sister, Mariza." He turned to Morgana.

Her face contorted, and the taste of bile coated her tongue.

"And look where that got me? Her stealing my plans on how I was going to kill you and using them for herself. Never mind. Didn't she use to be lovers with Gareth? So, in reality, we have had each other's sexual partners. What do they call it…" he tapped his chin, "… Oh yes, sloppy seconds?"

Morgana gritted her teeth and strained against the silver chains, trying to ignore the searing burn in her skin. She pushed forward, gathering up the little strength she had left. They would not hurt her friend.

The groaning of wood echoed all around them as she shifted forward a mere inch or less, but it was enough to garner Ragnorok's attention.

"How the fuck are you still able to move?" he cried, exasperated. "Gun!"

Taste of Revenge

Cedric ran up, aiming the gun at Morgana's heart. His finger moved to the trigger, but Ragnorok slapped his hand out of the way, and the bullet flew past her into one of the humans behind her. A low groan was heard.

"Idiot! I want her alive."

"But, boss—"

"She has to die *in front of her parents.* They have to watch the life leave her eyes as I had to endure watching Angelique die," Ragnorok cried in frustration, stomping up to Morgana's pool. At least Ava wasn't being harmed now. Ragnorok placed the gun up near her temple. "This is all your fault."

"Me?"

"Shut it for once, will you?!" Ragnorok waved the gun in her face. "If you hadn't killed Svetlana, this place wouldn't be going to the shit. She ran this place with an iron fist."

Morgana glanced to her side. Her eyes locked with Ava's widening eyes. They exchanged small smiles before looking away. Ragnorok's snarl drew her attention back to him.

"What's this?" he pointed back and forth between them. "Why are you looking at each other like that?"

Morgana's smile stretched further. Maybe it was time to inflict a little psychological torture back on the Forest Clan leader.

"As much as I'd like to take the credit for blondie's demise... no offense, Ava."

"None taken," said Ava.

"It wasn't me who killed her. Father did."

"The Primus killed her?" Ragnorok whispered, looking back and forth between them. Ava nodded.

"No!" Ragnorok howled, falling to his knees, grasping his head in his hands. "She was the one who was supposed to kill the Primus." Ragnorok's chest heaved before he stood back up, his pained face was turning into a scowl. "This changes nothing. I'm going to enjoy watching you die. Even more so now. And to watch Oscar and Vivienne fall to their knees at your death. And when the Primus is weakened by his grief, then I'll end him. The Daywalker's grief will be a delicious bonus."

"And when I kill you, I'm going to dance in your ashes," Morgana hissed.

"Not likely." Ragnorok aimed the gun at her stomach and fired once more.

"Morgana!" Ava cried.

"It's fine, Ava." Morgana slurred, the familiar blackness descending. There was some satisfaction in the knowledge they had to keep shooting her again and again to keep her down.

Taste of Revenge

The shrilling noise brought Morgana back to consciousness, and she lifted her head to find the source—Ava squirmed in her ropes, looking uncomfortable.

"What's that infernal racket?" Ragnorok snarled glancing between the two of them.

He walked over to Ava. "It's coming from you. What's that?" He reached into her sweater pocket and pulled out her cell phone.

"Ah, you little minx. You tried to call for help, did you?"

Ava raised an eyebrow. "How can I do that when my arms are tied?"

Ragnorok huffed, looking at the screen, which stopped but started to ring again. "It says Dad. Well now, this is interesting."

"You should answer it. Otherwise, he'll likely ping my phone for my whereabouts. Then he'll come looking for me. I haven't turned up to work today, which isn't like me, and I won't be at my apartment or Alastor's. He might even send the police."

"Let them come." Cedric piped up, "That'll bring fresh blood. The others are starting to get old."

Ragnorok looked at his new second-in-command. "Are you from this town? No?" Cedric shook his head. "I forget where I got you from. No, the local human authorities in this place are on the unhealthy-looking side. So that means their blood is unlikely to be tasty. What we want is fresh, vibrant young humans, like these two delicious morsels we have here." Ragnorok tapped the phone onto his open palm. "Though bringing the human authorities here, would likely bring The Council to me faster."

"Please," Ava begged, "Just let me answer it."

"No, it seems more fun to let you sweat and suffer. Though human sweat does taint the taste of blood, especially with the wolfsbane on your skin." Ragnorok stared at Ava. "Very well, I'll allow it… just to prove to the vampire killer over here that I'm not the blood-thirsty monster she thinks I am."

Morgana scowled.

Ragnorok held the phone up to Ava's ear while it was still ringing.

"You have to press the green phone on the screen," Ava told him.

Morgana burst into laughter, only stopping abruptly because the wounds in her torso hurt from the movement. Ragnorok glared at her before turning his attention back to the phone and pressing answer. "Like this?"

Ava nodded.

"Ava, honey, is that you?" a male voice on the other end said.

"Hi, Dad."

"Where have you been all day? I've been calling you nonstop."

"Sorry, didn't you get my email? I'm feeling under the weather. I think it might be the flu."

Ragnorok nodded in approval.

Morgana wanted to shout to Ava to tell him they'd been kidnapped, but she didn't want to put Ava's father in jeopardy or risk revealing vampires.

"No, I never received your email."

"Oh, I must have thought I sent it. My brain is a little fuzzy now."

"Do you need me to bring anything around for you?"

"No, I don't want you to catch it. I'm fine, anyway. Alastor is looking after me."

"Good to hear. Well, I hope you get better. I'm going to look into that old estate for any clues."

"No need," Ava spoke quickly. "I already looked there. If you go out there, it will be a dead end."

Clever girl, warning her father away from there.

"Are you sure? Sheriff Webster was so adamant there was something out there."

"No, just some teenagers using it as a party house on the weekends."

"Well, definitely no news story there, then. I'll keep digging. We'll find out who's taking these kids."

"Sure," Ava said weakly, her eyes darting to Ragnorok who had a wide, cruel grin on his face.

"Well, Dad, I better go. I need to rest now."

"Sure, honey. Rest up, and I'll see you in the office when you're all well again."

"Yep, sounds great."

Morgana closed her good eye. The phone call may have stopped Ava's father from going out to the old town lair, but that wouldn't stop Sheriff Webster from looking into it. She thought they'd been doing a terrific job keeping the police from knowing what was going on. Clearly, the façade was failing. Not only had she been caught, but she was also failing this mission. Her head hung low. Hopefully, the others were picking up the slack and were aware of the situation. If they were draining humans here, surely, they were doing it at the town lair. Maybe that's why they hadn't come for her yet. They were tying up loose ends.

Morgana lifted her head and opened her eye. Ragnorok was taking the phone away from Ava and looking at her with a raised brow. "Well?"

"Press the red button on the screen." She sniffled. A tear streaked down her cheek.

Ragnorok did as he was told before snapping the phone in two and throwing the pieces to the side.

"Hey! Those are expensive, you know." Ava's nostrils flared, and her hazel eyes glared at the Forest Clan leader. Quite brave, Morgana thought—*for someone about to be drained of every ounce of blood once the wolfsbane wore off her skin.*

Taste of Revenge

"At least it stopped you from crying," Ragnorok sneered. "The only thing worse tasting than human sweat getting into the blood is tears."

CHAPTER 35

Ava was not an overly religious person, partly because she enjoyed doing research and was always looking for concrete answers to her questions. Religion was just one of those things that had too many unanswered questions for her liking.

Regardless of her lack of faith, at that moment, she sent a prayer thanking the gods, fates, fairies, angels, unicorns, mermaids, or whomever it was that was looking out for her. She was also thankful for the wolfsbane on her skin, preventing Ragnorok and his minions from slicing into her and draining her like a cow in an abattoir.

"But, boss, wouldn't her sweat and tears wash away the wolfsbane on her skin?" the gangly looking vampire asked.

"Wash?" It was like the Forest Clan leader had never spoken the word before.

"Yeah, it's what humans do to get rid of the day's grime." The vampire snapped his fingers. "It's too bad we're not back at the town lair, we could have hosed her down."

"Ho-s-ed," the Forest Clan leader sounded out the word out.

"Yeah, maybe I could send some folks out to get buckets of water to dump on her."

"And this washing with buckets of water will rid her skin of the apotropaics?"

"Yeah, good idea," Morgana's croaky voice sounded behind them. "Fill her kiddie pool up with 'toxic' water before you drain her, then water down her blood with poison. Sounds delicious." Morgana tried to laugh but ended up choking instead.

Ava gave her a sympathetic look. Her friend had to be struggling. How horrible it must be to be alive but just barely.

Ragnorok hissed, "She's right." He pointed to the blue tub she stood in. "What do we do with the water that will run into the pool?"

"Why don't we take her out, wash her, the water falls to the ground, then we tie her back to the pole?" The gangly vampire glared at Morgana as he spoke.

Morgana shot daggers right back at him with her one eye.

"If it will speed up the process, then yes, proceed." Ragnorok waved his hand. He grinned and turned to Morgana. "Ready to watch your friend die?"

"Why not just wash her arms?" A vampire who looked like he hailed from the Viking era stepped forward. "That's the only part we need to cut... that and her thighs." He looked toward her legs. "She's wearing breeches. Surely, the wolfsbane wouldn't have touched her skin there."

"True, Nasir. I should have made you my second-in-command."

The gangly vampire opened his mouth, looking affronted but was silenced by a look from the Forest Clan leader.

Ava was untied from the pole. The vampires were careful not to touch her skin as they ripped the sleeves off her sweater. She tried to break free, but their grip was like steel vices around her torso and shoulders. Alastor had truly held back his strength whenever they embraced. The thought of her boyfriend made her heart ache. Oh, how she missed him. She was forced to bend forward in the kiddie pool, her arms straight out in front of her while wet cloths were scrubbed against her skin. Then she was straightened back up, and her body slammed against the pole. Her ankles, once again, were placed on either side of the pole, her arms tied behind her, hugging the pole. Her muscles strained and ached from the unnatural position.

Ragnorok brandished a knife, grinning at Morgana straining against the chains, her brown eyes blazing.

"Get ready," he crooned before slicing the tip of the blade in a diagonal slash across her left inner thigh. Ava screamed, tears brimming in her eyes. "Gah!" she cried, the blade slicing her other thigh. She howled. Thuds sounded as her blood dripped onto the plastic below.

"Ava!" Morgana rasped.

Ragnorok looked out the corner of his eye toward Morgana as he walked behind Ava.

"No more," she blubbered as the sharp metal tore into her flesh, slicing along the veins. Just when she thought she couldn't handle any more pain, a slap bloomed across her left cheek, sending her blurred vision sideways. She could just make out the other humans tied to their poles—lifeless, heads slumped forward.

"I thought I told you no tears in the blood," Ragnorok growled.

"She can't help it," Morgana grated. "It's a human hormonal reaction to emotions and pain. They have very little control over it, if any." Morgana could barely lift her head.

Ava looked up at Morgana, breathing through her tears. It was terrible seeing her friend this way. Open wounds were riddling her limp body. Morgana was like a ragdoll being held up by the very chains burning into her flesh, blood matting her body.

It was twisted and in years to come, the guilt of these thoughts would wake Ava up in the middle of the night, but as she gazed upon Morgana, she thought of her bloodletting wounds. She drew strength from the fact Morgana was far worse off.

CHAPTER 36

Gareth's eyes bulged watching the row of Primus entering the Van Wilden's living room. The presence they emitted was very old and powerful. He exchanged a look with Alastor before they stood flanking Mr. and Mrs. V, who had begun greeting each one as they entered. All their accents sounded like they were from some old European country. Gareth recalled something about Morgana saying the Primus Vampyr originated in the old country but over the years shifted to the different continents of the world.

"Is this him?" A frail-looking woman with bright hazel eyes and copper hair streaked with wisps of white walked up to him.

"Yes," someone answered.

Whack. Her hand met with the side of his face, snapping it to the side. He heard spitting, but his vision was dark with bright, colorful dots.

"Elder Gettybourgh, you will refrain from hitting Council employees," a deep voice boomed.

"He should be the one in jail," she spat. As his eyesight was clearing, he saw her raising her hand again. He cringed, waiting for the next slap.

"Gareth was suitably punished for his crime," Oscar said, making the female halt. "And as I recall, it was *your* son who went *rogue* attacking *my* wife, Gareth, Morgana, Alastor, and me."

"Refrain from hitting my future son-in-law any further from now on, Cleva." Vivienne walked up to them, her ice-blue eyes glaring at the female Elder.

Gareth's head jerked up. *Future son-in-law?* He must have missed something.

"Whoa... are you and my sis getting hitched?" Hector slapped him on the back again.

Gareth adjusted his jaw, snapping it back into place. "Ah, no."

Vivienne cleared her throat. "One day you'll marry into the family." She winked.

Gareth raised an eyebrow. "We *better* get Morgana back, then. Without her, my options for marrying into this family are less than enticing." He'd meant to lighten the mood, but glanced nervously at Morgana's brothers, realizing he may have just offended someone.

Jonas was stoic until Hector released a deep, guttural laugh.

Oscar chuckled, placing a hand on Gareth's shoulder. "Yes, I suppose marriage is the last thing we need to think about right this second. Are you sure you're okay, son?"

It was starting to make sense why Oscar kept calling him son. Gareth tested his jaw. "Yeah, it's fine." He watched the female Elder grumbling to herself while walking to the other side of the room. She glanced back a few times, shooting him evil looks.

"Old woman Gettybourgh, Randalf's mother," Hector told him.

"Yeah, I caught that." Gareth made a mental note to stay away from her during the battle. *In case she tried to stake him.* "Why is she here, then?"

"She has a soft spot for Morgana. Took it hard when things didn't work out between Morgana and her son."

Jonas walked up and handed him a tumbler of blood. "Looks like you could do with this."

Gareth took it from him, smiling. "Thanks, you're a champ. So, who else do we have here?"

Jonas took a sip from his glass of blood and turned around, facing the room. "Well, the two gorgeous ladies to your left are Jelani of the Kalu coven..." Jonas pointed with his glass in an uncanny resemblance to Oscar, toward a beautiful dark-skinned woman with high cheekbones and onyx eyes. She winked at him. "Next to her is Agnor of the

Eydis coven." The woman standing next to Jelani had ash blonde hair and gray-blue eyes. She gave a little finger wave at the mention of her. "Both are matriarchs of their covens, and two quite powerful women."

Hector snorted. "You're just saying that because you're banging Eshe."

"Whose Eshe? Is she here?" Gareth looked around the room.

"Jelani's daughter, and no, she's not here. She's out on a mission."

Hector added, "Jonas' fuck buddy."

Jonas shook his head, but his lips were twitching. "I prefer the term *part-time lover*." He took another sip of blood. "Fuck buddy just sounds so crass. She's more to me than that."

"Well, brother dear, why don't you step things up with her, then? You've both been like this for three thousand years."

"Yes, when are you going to marry my daughter?" Jelani raised an eyebrow.

"You both know I can't."

"Aye?" Alastor piped up.

"It's difficult to maintain a relationship between agents. What with being assigned to different parts of the world for however long each mission takes. We've just kept it simple."

"Oh." Gareth hadn't thought much about how his and Morgana's relationship would go after this mission had ended. Where would it leave them?

"Don't worry about you and Morgana. You guys have your bond. You should get assigned together. Most married vampires work well together as a team. You both know what each other is feeling and know where they are at all times."

"Yeah, except for when I couldn't feel her."

"True." Jonas patted him on the back. "But you know where she is now. That's all that matters. And when you're in the field, you'll have each other's back."

Gareth hoped so. After this ordeal, he never wanted to be separated from Morgana again.

"I wish I had someone in my life who cared about me as much as you do, young Gareth, for Morgana," Agnor said.

"You know I'd shag ya, Agnor, if you'd let me." Hector waggled his eyebrows.

"You know you aren't too old to receive a good boxing around the ears, young Hector." Agnor shook her finger at him.

"Hey, you may act like an old matriarch, but you're about as youthful as I am. You're like a GILF."

"A what now?" Gareth said.

"Grandmother, I'd like to fuck." Hector grinned.

Agnor stepped forward, holding onto her skirts with a scowl on her face.

Jelani placed a hand on her arm. "You know Hector's just trying to goad you, Agnor."

Agnor's scowl deepened as she shook her finger at Hector in warning.

Hector put his palms up backing away but smirking.

Gareth looked between the two of them. "Has anyone actually done that before? Been romantic with an Elder?"

"Nah," Hector said. "I joke around to stir up old Agnor, but it would be like banging your grandma. Can you imagine someone of our generation getting with say, someone like old Batheras over there? Yeesh."

Jonas and two other male Primus chuckled while Batheras frowned. "These two gentlemen laughing at my brother is the Elder of the Hammadi coven." Jonas pointed to a bald vampire with copper skin and deep brown eyes, who nodded his head in their direction.

"We nicknamed him Anubi," Hector muttered to Gareth and Alastor. "Anubis was the human God associated with death in Egypt. You get it... death, vampires, and the role we play?" He winked at them both.

Gareth's mouth twitched, and Alastor had to cover his mouth to stifle his laugh. Now was not the time to laugh at Council Elders.

Taste of Revenge

Jonas shook his head and continued with his introductions. "Elder Gregorus of the Olderman coven."

"It is nice to meet you both." Gregorus stepped forward, speaking in the same accent all the Elders spoke with. He smiled at them, his deep-set brown eyes were filled with warmth as he held out his hand.

Gareth took his hand to shake, trying not to flinch from the strength of his grip. He'd forgotten they were all so much stronger than him.

"Sorry about that." Gregorus withdrew his hand. "From the reports we've received, I tend to forget you're human-turned."

"Yes, you have both been proving to be valuable additions to The Council of Order," spoke the frowning sandy-haired Primus with the deep booming voice who had commanded Cleva to stop slapping Gareth earlier. Now his odd, teal-colored eyes scrutinized them both.

"And as you may have guessed by now, this is our fearless leader of the Batheras coven." Jonas continued, "It was Batheras who came up with the idea of The Council of Order."

"Yes, well, something had to be done." He nodded to Gareth and Alastor before entering into a conversation with Oscar.

"Batheras' first name is the same as the family coven name?"

"For the longest time, we didn't use surnames. That only began when we decided to integrate into human society. So, a lot of the coven names were taken after their leader."

"Aye, makes sense," Alastor commented.

"So what have you guys nicknamed him, then?"

Jonas and Hector exchanged amused looks before answering at the same time, "Archi."

"But don't let him hear you calling him that." Hector turned his back to the crowd, keeping his voice low so only Gareth and Alastor could hear.

"Who is she, then?" Gareth looked toward a small woman with jet black hair sitting quietly in the remaining armchair.

"Elder Eleanor of the Wellchide coven."

She turned at the mention of her name, giving them a small smile.

"And the rest?" There were many more vampires moving and shifting furniture around.

"More agents of The Council like Hector and I. They're children and grandchildren of the Elders here. Gregorus and Hammadi even share a granddaughter."

"Who?"

"My PA, Clarita."

"Is she here?"

Gareth scanned the Primus to see if he could spot a new face.

Taste of Revenge

"No, she chose to stay behind and keep things running for me while I'm here. I've still got some other agents out in the field."

"Grandchildren?" Gareth asked. "But I thought you all stopped breeding after a couple of generations?"

"Most of us did. It would have started becoming incestual."

"And confusing," Hector muttered.

"Confusing how?" Alastor asked.

"With no one quite sure who was belonging to which coven anymore," Jonas answered. "Take for example, one of Agnor's granddaughters, Dontelle, and while she has an amicable relationship with her grandmother, she belongs to the Olderman coven. Agnor's daughter, Cabrini married Gregorus' son, Ezra, and entered the Oldermans.

"Then you have Ohana's daughter joining the Wellchides. Do you see the two Primus there with Eleanor?"

Gareth nodded.

"That's her son, Hadwyne, and Kaiya, his mate." A petite young woman with large almond eyes and the stoic man standing next to her with a mop of unruly black hair smiled at him.

"They're not married?"

"Yeah, they used to be the same as you and Morgs, but it's only just recently they decided to tie the knot," said Hector.

"Ah yes, they did, too. Elder Wellchide's other two daughters are back at Headquarters. Neither are married or with mates," Jonas added.

"So, is it only the women who marry or join into other covens?"

"No. Cleva's first son, Palmar, married Alexandria—"

"Don't let her hear you call her by that name, though, bro," Hector interjected.

Jonas shot his brother a look but kept talking, "Batheras' daughter and became part of their coven."

"But when you meet Xandria, you'll understand why," Hector joked.

"Agnor's second son, Endre, also married into another coven to Hammadi's daughter, Persiphine." Jonas pointed to a petite copper-skinned beauty with wide almond eyes. She nodded at them.

"And what about you lot? Didn't marry or mate with any others?"

Hector coughed. "Nah, us Van Wilden children have always been lone wolves, so to speak. Well, until you and Morgs shacked up."

"That's not entirely true," Jonas muttered.

"Aye, we all know how Mariza worked," Alastor commented dryly.

"Yeah, it was also quite the surprise when old Randy first asked Morgana to marry him. But I think he just wanted her to join the Gettybourgh coven."

Gareth arched an eyebrow. "Well, clearly he didn't know her all that well because she'd have never done that, especially since I'm the one to have joined the Van Wildens."

Hector guffawed and slapped him on the back, earning him another dark look from Cleva.

"What happened to all these spouses?"

"The war," Jonas said quietly. "It was after the war that family coven pride became more prominent."

"Agnor lost all of her children and her husband, making her a coven of one."

"But doesn't coven usually mean a group?"

Agnor was in front of him before he knew it. Gareth cringed anticipating a snap from another Primus Elder.

"As young Jonas said, family pride is keeping my family name alive."

Gareth tilted his head. "You kinda sound like Ragnorok," he blurted out.

"Not surprising. All the Elders and their children are from the old country."

"But you all look so—"

"Diverse?"

"Well, yeah." He rubbed the back of his neck.

"Remember, we were alive before the human civilizations that are in place now. We have never seen each other as being different because of our different features. It was always us Primus Vampyr against the humans before we eventually integrated into the different races."

Gareth nodded.

"I do regret this has happened, old friend." Hammadi squeezed Oscar's shoulder.

"We're all very sorry for what has happened to Morgana, Octavius."

"Well, if you hadn't taken so long to make a decision, Ragnorok might not have taken Morgana or Ava," Gareth muttered.

Batheras stared him down. Jesus, did all the Primus learn how to perfect that stare together?

"This mission has had unusual circumstances right from the beginning with Oscar recruiting human-turned vampires, to one of our own going rogue and attacking you all." His eyes flickered to Cleva, who was staring hard at the wall—her mouth twisted as she tugged on her red, beaded necklace.

"Young man, we don't decide to end any vampire's life lightly." Jelani glowered at him. "We've all experienced what loss feels like, so we take our time to assess whether it is necessary to do so. Regardless of whether they are being—"

"Insolent little pricks?" Agnor offered.

Jelani's lips twitched. "I'd have offered another name for them." She turned to her friend, shaking her head.

"Besides," Gregorus spoke before Jelani could continue, "Yours isn't the only mission we have to make decisions on. We're in touch with every vampire group in every country all around the planet."

"It's a lot of lives to consider." Jelani locked her brown eyes with Gareth's.

Jonas squeezed Gareth's shoulder. "We get it that you're angry. We all want Morgana and Ava back. That's why we're all here."

"Fine," Gareth mumbled.

"Right, if we could proceed with the meeting," Oscar said, his voice stern, making Gareth raise his chin to meet the Elder, his coven leader, and possibly his future father-in-law dead in the eyes. Oscar's brown eyes were full of understanding. A fierce determination spread through his body.

"Tell us the plan, boss."

CHAPTER 37

The Van Wilden's dining table had been shifted into the living room, and the vampires spread themselves around it as best they could. The large map of the area was spread across the top. There were now extra markings on the paper from the intel gathered by Jonas and Hector.

"The girls and the other humans are being kept here." Oscar tapped a section of the map. The Forest Clan had their homes spread out in a semi-circle surrounding what they'd marked as the 'feeding area,' the clearing where Morgana, Ava, and the other humans were being held. According to Jonas and Hector's reports, they were being strapped to poles in kiddie pools and being drained of their blood. Gareth curled his lip up in disgust at the thought. Not the most hygienic way to store blood.

"So, Pops, what's the plan?" Hector asked.

Taste of Revenge

"No more picking off the Forest Clan one by one. I erred in judgment by ordering us to do so. We eradicate them. Every single member of that clan."

"Aye, and the humans they're using as a food source?" Alastor asked.

"Unfortunately, they will be collateral damage. We can't rescue them only to have them tell of their ordeals regarding vampires to others."

"What if no one believes them?" Gareth spoke up.

"We can't risk it."

"Ava is the only human we rescue. Understood?" Oscar said sternly, looking toward his sons.

Gareth furrowed his brow. What was *that* about?

"Of course," both Jonas and Hector agreed.

"So, the strategy of attack?"

"We strike from the front taking down the dwellings in your wake as well. Use the broken wood to your advantage, too. From the numbers we've received, we might not be able to carry that many stakes on us."

"What about the vampire lore about the stakes needing to have a special ritual placed on them?" Gareth knew all about this from his punishment for staking Randalf. He and Morgana had to whittle thousands upon thousands of stakes to send to other agents. He was going to be more pissed off than he already was if that were not the case.

"He has a point." Hammadi stroked his chin.

"We'll burn all the bodies together."

"Or with all us Elders here we can bless the wood?" offered Elder Wellchide.

"Very well. But it will have to be quick."

Elder Wellchide raised an eyebrow. *Nothing could beat the speed of a Primus Vampyr.*

Oscar chuckled. "You know very well what I meant, Eleanor."

She nodded, her eyes twinkling with mirth.

"We go in, eradicate the Forest Clan, and free the girls. Are we all clear on this?"

"I think Morgana will want to be part of the fight, too," Gareth argued.

"True." Oscar tapped his index finger on the map. "We split into two groups, then. Gareth, Alastor, and Vivienne you rescue the girls. Morgana will be weak, so you'll need to remove her from the battle to tend to her wounds. You and Vivienne should both give her blood, so neither of you are depleted too much. That way she'll be able to join in."

Gareth nodded.

"Then come back with her and join us in the fight."

"The rest of us will still attack from the front, drawing the attention away from the rescue."

"Well, it is The Council that this Ragnorok fellow wants to take down. So, it's the full force of The Council he will get," Batheras' booming voice reverberated around the room.

"Jonas and I will go with the rescue party," Hector said. "We came here to rescue our sis, and that's what we're going to do."

Vivienne flashed them a grin, respect in her eyes for her stepsons.

Gareth would eventually find out what the backstory was there.

"Good, then it's settled." Oscar moved to stand in front of the fireplace, turned to face all of them and cleared his throat.

A female vampire, whose name Gareth couldn't remember, was handing out shot glasses of blood. She gave a flirtatious smile to Gareth when she approached him. Sure, she was pretty with her olive skin and bright green eyes rimmed with a forest green color, but she was also a blonde, and he'd had enough of them.

They were also there to rescue his *girlfriend*. Gareth scowled at her before taking his glass.

Hector nudged him. "Don't stress on it, bro. Dontelle flirts with everyone." Hector watched her ass as she sashayed around the room.

"Yes, but if I recall correctly, you're the only one who has responded," Jonas muttered.

"Yeah, of course, I tapped that." Hector slapped him on the shoulder, "Besides, you're practically engaged if Viv has her way."

Despite his sour mood, Gareth found himself smiling at Hector.

"I like you, Hector," Gareth told him. "I was a bit wary of meeting Morgana's other siblings."

Hector let out a loud laugh. "Not all of us are like old Riza." Hector tipped his chin to his brother. "Jonas is pretty cool, too."

Jonas smiled but kept his eyes to the front, looking at his father.

Oscar cleared his throat. "Thank you all for taking the time to come here and address this new threat to our society. And to help rescue my daughter and a special honorary member of my coven, Ava, who, as she's spent more time with us in our world, I've come to think of as a third daughter."

Alastor nodded his thanks and raised his glass to Oscar, who nodded his head in return. "They also took the life of someone very dear to me, Brutus, my little buddy. He was more than just a pet, he was my companion."

Gareth wanted to shed a tear for Brutus. He had been an awesome dog in the short time they'd known him.

"They took something precious to us, but we'll take something even more precious to them… their lives. Tonight, we take down Ragnorok and his Forest Clan once and for all, sending a message to our brethren across the world. Anyone who messes with The Council of Order is going to get their ass handed to them."

Gareth's jaw dropped.

"Jaysus," Alastor muttered beside him.

But no one else seemed to react. Maybe Oscar wasn't all that prim and proper.

Oscar raised his shot glass calling out, "*Ladas kampfet ne viri numar att lag famil!*"

The Primus in the room lifted their glasses. "*Viri numar ne famil!*" they chorused before downing their shot glasses of blood.

Gareth and Alastor exchanged looks before repeating the same actions.

"What did Oscar say at the end?" Gareth asked Jonas.

Jonas looked at him, giving him the Van Wilden stare. "It's the language of the old country. "*There's strength in fighting alongside your coven, your family*." And we replied, "*To fighting with family*." Jonas clapped Gareth on the back before walking down to the basement.

The knowledge that each Primus was here fighting for Morgana and Ava caused Gareth's throat to constrict, stopping the flow of blood sliding down.

"You're not getting teary on us, are you, bro?" Hector thumped him on his back.

Gareth shook his head and held up his hand as he swallowed. "I'm fine." He gave them a tight-lipped smile and stood straight. He looked around the room, his smile growing genuine. Not only were each Primus—well, except Cleva—here for them, but for Alastor too. They were all his family now.

CHAPTER 38

With so many mouths to feed for the big battle, Gareth and Alastor opted to take Morgana's brothers and a few of the younger generation Primus to feed at their place. The Van Wilden's fridge was running low, but Vivienne had often made sure to use their blood supply connections to keep Gareth and Alastor's fridge fully stocked.

Hector whistled low while looking around their foyer when they entered. "Sweet digs."

Gareth barely nodded. He could feel Alastor's eyes on him, but he couldn't look at his best friend right now.

"Aye, the kitchen is this way, lads and lasses." Alastor led them away.

Gareth didn't feel like following, he just wanted a moment to be alone. "I'm going upstairs to change," he called out as an excuse, already ascending the stairs.

When he entered his room, he stopped at the base of the bed, staring at the bite mark Morgana had left. With all that had been going on since that night, he'd never had the chance to replace his mattress. That night all he'd thought about was getting his rocks off. If he had known what was to come, he would have made love to her and not taken her so roughly.

"Ye all right, mate?" Alastor's hand clamped down on his shoulder, startling him from his thoughts, making him jump to the side a few paces.

"Jesus, you're good at sneaking up on people."

"Aye." Alastor winked at him. *"Stealth training."*

Gareth nodded. A few weeks back Vivienne had taken Alastor under her wings and began training him in stealth techniques that later enabled him to sneak up on Mariza and kill—no stake—her. Geez, he still had to get his head around the fact that his creator was still alive.

"How are ye feelin'?"

"I should probably be asking you the same thing."

"Shithouse."

Gareth grinned. "Yep, that about sums it up."

"Aye." Alastor started to chuckle but cut himself short. "Seems wrong to laugh when the lasses are, ye know?"

Gareth scrubbed the back of his neck. "Yeah, I know."

Taste of Revenge

The sounds of the vampires below drifted up through the floorboards.

"But we're not alone. We've got that lot helping us out. *Viri numar ne famil*," Gareth repeated the earlier sentiment.

"Aye, but *ye know* that Morgana is still alive. I don't know about Ava."

Gareth gave his friend a sympathetic look. "She might still be. They kept the humans alive in the town lair for the uninvited barrier protection. They could be using Ava in a similar way."

"Well, as sick as it may sound, that gives me hope."

"Then use that hope to fuel you... to go get her."

"Aye."

"Oi, are you two bozos eating, or can we have your share?" Hector called out to them.

"Ignore him," Jonas called out. The sounds of a slap to the back of the head could be heard.

Gareth and Alastor looked at each other before laughing. "We better get down there and feed before Hector drinks it all."

"Aye, if Mrs. V found out we didn't eat up before the battle... well, I don't want to find out."

Gareth grinned, slapping his friend playfully on the back as they walked out of the room.

It was time to get the girls.

CHAPTER 39

Oscar sat in his armchair watching his wife, always the gracious host, flitting around handing glasses of blood around to the others. His eyes squinted when he noticed some of his whiskey glasses were being used.

"Excuse me," he said to the other Elders before following her back into the kitchen. She was busy, emptying blood bags into fresh glasses. Oscar walked around the island counter, placing a hand on her arm, stilling her movements.

"Here, let me do that, dear. You've been doing quite a lot recently."

She shook her head, resuming her task. "No, it's fine." She sighed. "Doing this, cleaning up sites and porches, keeps me busy and my mind off—"

Oscar's grip tightened slightly but not enough to hurt her. "I'm sorry, my dear, with you caring for everyone and handling Gareth and Alastor, I never asked you how your grief is going."

Vivienne emptied the last drops of blood before looking up at him. "You know how I'm feeling."

"Ah, but it's a husband's job to ask his wife how she is rather than taking the bond for granted."

Vivienne dropped the bag onto the marble countertop. She wiped her hand on a tea towel, her movements slow and methodical. He could feel her sorting out her feelings through the bond. She turned to him and touched his face. "I'll be fine, eventually. Once we get this lot fed and armed as best we can, so we can go rescue the girls," a fierce determination passed over her face and through the bond, "and we do what we agents of The Council do best... eradicate that smug, evil bastard."

Oscar nodded, cupping her cheek. "Yes, we will." His hand dropped, and he turned back to face the counter, leaning his hands on it, keeping his voice low, so the others wouldn't catch wind of what he was about to say next. "I guess that means I can no longer pretend to be human anymore?"

Vivienne's voice grew soft, and sympathy flowed from her. "No, not for the rest of the mission, and maybe even for a while after that. Morgana will need her father to be his Primus Vampyr self so we can take down the Forest Clan, bring her home, and help her to rehabilitate from whatever horrors they've put her through."

Oscar looked up, meeting his wife's icy-blue eyes. He turned back to her, smiling and placing his hand under her chin. "Always the clever one." He pressed his lips to hers. They pulled apart, resting their foreheads against each other. They allowed themselves this moment before Vivienne pulled back, her determination once again settling in. "Well, I better get this blood distributed so that we can get our daughter back."

Oscar nodded and watched her exit the room, his hip resting on the island counter. He looked down at the empty blood bags littering the counter.

This was no time to wallow in his grief and anguish. It was time to get his daughter and Ava.

It was time for Ragnorok and his Forest Clan to pay.

For he was Octavius Van Wilden.

A Primus Vampyr—one of the eldest of all the vampires.

And he was going to kill them all.

CHAPTER 40

Gareth crept up to the shrubbery surrounding the clearing. From his crouched position, he could see Morgana slumped against a pole, the silver chains binding her were the only things holding her upright.

The smell of her blood was wafting all around him. There were open wounds all over her body, her blood was seeping out.

He thought he was angry before, but now his blood boiled with his rage.

The one thing Morgana didn't want to be in her life—a blood bag—and Ragnorok did exactly that to her.

He was also shocked by the possessiveness he felt at the thought of others drinking her blood. That blood was his.

Morgana was his.

If anyone were going to drink her blood, it would be him.

Jealousy was a strong emotion. She must have felt him. She looked right at him even though he was hidden.

All the jealousy burned away by the anger at seeing her forlorn face. One brown eye was straining toward him. The other enclosed in a mass of swollen purple bruising.

That fucker was going to pay.

Gareth saw Ragnorok standing over her. He could hear him gloating. Gareth prepared himself to run into the clearing, but a hand grabbed his shoulder.

Gareth looked to the owner of the hand in surprise. It was Oscar. He pressed a finger to his lips. There were so many vampires around, it wasn't a wonder he hadn't sensed *him*.

Gareth pointed to the scene through the leaves and went to make a move again. Oscar shook his head, mouthing at Gareth to step away.

He shook his head. *Fuck that*. His mate was *right there*. He needed to rescue her. Gareth moved to leap, but a hand covered his mouth, pulling him back. Gareth struggled to fight against Oscar. It was like steel had been wrapped around his body. Oscar dragged Gareth away from the clearing. They entered an area out of earshot to the Forest Clan. Oscar released Gareth.

Taste of Revenge

"What are you doing?" Gareth snapped. "He has Morgana back there."

"Patience, young man," Batheras spoke to his left. Out of the shadows emerged the Council Elders. Batheras stepped forward where Oscar and Gareth were standing.

"Remember the plan, young whelp," Agnor said in her strong, commanding voice.

"We all need to be careful," Jelani commented. "Remember, Ragnorok has discovered the way to kill Primus."

"He's an arrogant young fool," Agnor scoffed. "There's no way he can beat us all."

"True," Batheras said. "But we have not survived for five-thousand years without knowing how to fight. We eradicate this so-called Ragnorok before he spreads through the country any further. Are we ready to battle, fellow Elders and agents?"

"Yes," came the reply in perfect chorus.

"Then the battle shall begin."

"I suggest you duck, Gareth." Oscar pulled him down, so he was squatting next to the Elder. Whistling noises rent through the air as flaming stakes sailed overhead, felling the guards and many Forest Clan vampires.

Then the alarm sounded as their enemy began to discover they were under attack.

"Time to move, everybody!" Jonas leaped up and headed toward the feeding area.

Gareth felt another tug on his arm. He turned to see Vivienne standing there with Alastor next to her.

Vivienne placed a hand on each of their cheeks. "Before you go in there, I just want to say… I'm so proud of both of you. Remember what I've trained you to do." She looked at each of them. "Come, let's go get our girls."

They crept quickly around the perimeter of the Forest Clan's lair, heading in the direction of where the girls were being held.

Gareth wasted no more time in getting to Morgana as his feet sloshed through the pool of blood at her feet. He grasped her face in his hands. "Morgana." A sudden giddiness swept over him at being able to touch her again.

"Gareth," her voice was weak but hopeful.

"Yes, I'm here."

Her eyes dropped. "No, you're not here. My mind is just conjuring the image of you standing there."

"Morgana, of course, I'm here."

Her head shook slightly.

"Does this feel real?" he gingerly lifted her face to look into his eyes, careful not to touch the bruised areas. He placed his lips onto hers, soft at first, his lips caressed hers, before his excitement at feeling and tasting her lips again overwhelmed him. He flicked his tongue against her lips, hoping she'd let him in. Her mouth parted, and he delved inside. Her tongue was dry from dehydration but all that mattered at this moment was proving he was here with her. He pulled back, searching her chocolate brown eyes for any recognition.

She looked at him, her eyes widening. "Gareth?" she whispered, "It's really you?"

"Yes, my love, it's me."

Joy and relief flooded through the bond.

Gareth searched her body. "Did he touch you anywhere else?"

"No. He said it would be like fucking a cow."

"You know, I've heard some humans do that."

Morgana laughed, but it turned into a gurgle as blood spilled from her mouth.

"Morgana!" he panicked, "Are you all right?"

She shook her head, and he wiped the blood away from her mouth, the excess dripped into the puddle at their feet.

He looked down. "Such a fucking waste," he muttered.

"Are you jealous, Gareth Lloyd?" Morgana asked, her voice raspy.

"Of course," he growled, "All of this is mine. If anyone were to drink from you, it was to be me. And me only."

Morgana grimaced. "Please no more talk of drinking from me. I've had enough to last a lifetime."

"Fair enough."

"I'm so ready to be free of here."

"And you will be."

A throat cleared behind him and he turned around to be face to face with Ragnorok.

"Unfortunately, for you, none of you will be leaving here alive."

As soon as they had approached the girls, Alastor ran toward Ava despite Vivienne's hand reaching out to slow him.

He didn't care if he were rushing into a trap. He needed to see if his girlfriend was all right.

"Ava." He cupped her face in his palms, his heart beating at the joy of seeing her.

"Alastor?" her voice was weak and raspy.

"Aye, lass."

A tear slid down her cheek. "Oh, thank God."

Alastor smiled.

Ava's hazel eyes gazed into his. "I'm so grateful now that you never bit me. Losing blood sucks."

Alastor, despite the situation, found himself chuckling. "Aye, lass, that's what us vampires do. We suck." He pressed his forehead to hers before pulling back.

"Look out!" Ava shouted.

Taste of Revenge

Alastor looked up in time to see a vampire dropping from the trees toward him.

CHAPTER 41

"You bastard," Gareth hollered, crash tackling into Ragnorok, slamming him into the dirt. His fists pummeled down on the clan leader's face. Ragnorok may have consumed Morgana's blood, but anger fueled his strength. "I'll fucking kill you for what you did to her."

He kept hitting until Ragnorok's face was a bloodied mess. He hadn't killed him, not by a long shot, but it still felt good.

His fists were a blur as he kept going. He groaned as he felt a stake impaling in his back, breaking his bloodlust. *Shit, where had that come from?* It wasn't in his heart, thank goodness, but it was piercing his spine. He angled his arms around his back to try to pull it out, his body contorting into different angles. Ragnorok groaned underneath him. He finally managed to grasp and yank the weapon out, throwing it to the ground.

Taste of Revenge

Gareth lifted himself off Ragnorok, spinning around to face the stake thrower.

All around him a battle was ensuing, not just where the Primus were fighting but here in the feeding grounds—his teammates fighting against the Forest Clan vampires.

Hector and Jonas worked as a synchronized pair. Hector punched a vampire with such force it propelled him backward. Jonas caught the flying vampire with one hand and, with the other, staked the vampire's heart through his back with such force the tip protruded through his ribs. Then, still holding the vampire up, he lit the end of the stake dropping the flaming vampire to the ground before turning to attack the next.

Gareth turned back around to see Ragnorok had gone. From the blood trail and the drag marks in the dirt, someone else had taken him away. He gritted his teeth and followed the vampire's scent to a hut, ducking and weaving through the chaos of fighting vampires. Gareth reached the hut only to hit an invisible wall when he couldn't go in. *Of course, the fucker would have a human living in there with him.* He slammed the invisible wall in frustration, seeing Ragnorok laid out on a crude-looking cot, vulnerable and ready to be killed. A gangly vampire appeared in the doorway grinning at him.

"Assholes," Gareth hissed before turning back to the fight. Ragnorok would heal soon enough and would likely join in. That was when Gareth would strike him again.

Irritation spiked through the bond, and he could feel Morgana's eyes on him. *Shit,* Morgana. He rubbed the back of his neck—what kind of mate was he, charging off and leaving her strapped to the pole? Yeah, he was definitely not going to win any boyfriend-of-the-year award.

He tried to duck and weave his way through, but with the huge battles raging on between him and her, it was clear he was going to have to fight his way back to her.

Alastor felt the vampire behind him even before Ava screamed out, and he twisted his torso in time, away from the vampire's arm swinging toward him, stake in hand. Alastor grabbed the offending arm and twisted it back against its owner, the vampire's blue-gray eyes widened as Alastor forced the stake into its owner's chest. He dropped the dead vampire to the ground, pulling his lighter free from his pocket to set the weapon alight.

He had no time to check if the body caught on fire as he was descended upon by more Forest Clan vampires.

"Feckin' bastards." He stood, rolling his neck. His hands moved to his stake holster before he stopped.

Taste of Revenge

Nay, he was going to fuck these bastards up using his bare hands. Then stake the assholes.

His fist slammed into the first vampire's face to approach him. The vampire stepped back before another stepped in. Alastor ducked the offending arm, ramming his shoulder into his attacker's stomach and pushed him back. He was trying to keep them away from Ava. A third was on him before he could recover. Alastor swung his fist into the vampire's stomach and staked him through the back as he was doubled over.

"Are ye all right, love?" He hopped from one foot to another watching the two vampires approach. He grasped two stakes in his hands. May as well end them. They hurtled toward him. As they neared, he swung to the side, tossing a stake at the left vampire, felling him in his tracks. The second vampire only had a second to look astonished at his clan member before he too was struck with a flying stake.

Alastor glanced at Ava.

"I'm fine. Just keep fighting."

"I'll free ye in a second."

"It's fine. I'm probably safer tied up here than being out there."

"Aye. True."

More vampires kept dropping from the trees, landing around them, eyes blazing with fury.

"They must be hungry," Ava commented.

Alastor nodded, though his lips twitched. They were, after all, freeing their food supply. Though, who knew what the other agents were doing to the other humans in the feeding area? The order was given not to let them live.

Alastor ducked as a vampire leaped toward him, fangs bared. The vampire sailed over his head, tumbling into the edge of Ava's kiddie pool.

Alastor swung around on his heel while still crouched, staking the vampire in his back before he could recover from his misplaced landing.

"Incoming!" someone yelled as another wave of Forest Clan vampires dropped from the trees.

Bloody hell. Where the feck did he recruit all of them from?

The loud, splintering noises of the huts being destroyed to his right drew his attention.

Oscar's team was shredding the wooden buildings and flinging the pieces of wood at the falling vampires. Grunts were heard as they hit their marks.

One of the Primus—he was pretty sure was Gregorus' grandson, Nardo—was swinging one of the wooden poles with frayed pieces of rope still hanging from it. He didn't want to know what happened to the human. Nardo swung the pole, hitting the vampires into the path of his sister who was catching and staking them like some sort of team sport. He shook his head in amazement. The last he counted before he was set upon again, the brother and sister team were up to four.

"Jaysus."

"Just keep fighting," Vivienne yelled.

Vivienne was holding her own. The blonde vampire swung her fists at one vampire, then turned to the attacking vampire behind her. She simultaneously staked both vampires in the chest.

He smiled. It never ceased to amaze him seeing how badass Mrs. V was.

Ragnorok stepped out of the hut, fully recovered from the Daywalker's beating. The half-breed's blood was amazing. The scene that met him was chaos and bedlam. The Primus were out for blood leaving none of his Forest Clan vampires alive in their path.

This was not how he had hoped this would go. His Forest Clan vampires appeared to be uncoordinated, unskilled, and undisciplined fighters. He growled, grabbing Cedric by his t-shirt collar. "Why aren't we using the hawthorn stakes against them?"

"Uh..." Cedric stammered, "They took us by surprise."

"How?" Ragnorok growled. "We've been planning this for years!" He pushed Cedric aside.

Angelique had been planning this even before he and Svetlana had taken her place. "Get the hawthorn stakes." He turned to Cedric, glaring when his second-in-command stood still. "Now!" he thundered.

Cedric scrambled off to retrieve the weapons.

His eyes cast to Morgana. Now that the huts were being torn down around the feeding area, he had a direct line of sight.

She glanced his way. Her one eye full of venom.

Ragnorok smiled. She was still chained to the pole. Good. He touched the hawthorn stake at his hip. There was still a way to get his vengeance.

CHAPTER 42

Oscar watched his family members creep away from him before joining in the fray, a stake in each hand.

While Ragnorok had amassed a huge army outnumbering them ten to one, most of them were newly-turned and no match for the power and speed of the Primus. They tore through the Forest Clan ranks, wrenching limbs from torsos and staking hearts. The agents followed them lighting the embedded stakes, leaving piles of ashes in their wake.

He had not been in a good brawl for years. This mission had certainly turned out to be an interesting yet bittersweet one.

So far, the Primus were winning the battle against the Forest Clan. Ragnorok's mistake had been to turn humans who were too young for maximum physical strength, and nowhere near old enough in their vampire existence. Compared to the strength and might of the Primus, Ragnorok was sending goats to the slaughter.

Oscar turned around to come face to face with one such youth. A young female vampire, her appearance and attire completely modern with her straight chestnut hair down to her white-tipped fingernails. He tilted his head, there was a familiarity about her like he'd seen this girl somewhere before.

Her soft brown eyes widened, and she fell to her knees. "I'm sorry."

They were in the middle of a battlefield, but Oscar placed a hand on her shoulder. "For what, child?"

She looked up, her eyes rimmed with red from tearless sobs. "I thought I wanted this. This type of existence. Because, you know, my boyfriend, Cedric, he became one." Her voice grew ragged. "But what they made me do, to him, to Brutus, it wasn't worth it."

Oscar's grip tightened on the girl's shoulders at the mention of his dead pet.

The girl squirmed and grunted, "You didn't kill my dog, though. I felt Ragnorok's presence all around him."

"No, but I may as well have." Her eyes captured his full attention. "I lured him outside."

Taste of Revenge

Oscar's roar rang all around them, and he lifted the girl still grasping her shoulder. His left hand shot out and grabbed her by the throat.

Her frightened cries were cut off by his hand constricting her throat. This girl had been part of the group who killed Brutus. *She should die.*

But as he stared at the girl dangling before him, her face turning purple, he realized if he killed her, any semblance of humanity he may have possessed would be shredded altogether. Her vampireness had barely begun. She'd done wicked things as a human, but he'd only be punishing the vampire. At the same time, she was a Forest Clan vampire and needed to be eradicated.

The girl gurgled. His contemplation had lasted far too long on a battlefield. Suddenly, a stake tip protruded from the front of her chest. He watched as the already dim light in her eyes flickered briefly, then disappeared. Dropping her limp body, he saw his wife standing before him with a cocky smile—a lighter in her hand.

"Darling, I thought you were fighting near the children?"

Vivienne raised an eyebrow. "A lady can run, dear."

"Thank you." He nodded toward the girl's crumpled body between them.

"I felt your rage and then your hesitancy." She stepped over the body, leaning close to him. "Don't worry about hesitating. She had to die. Brutus was my baby, too."

Oscar furrowed his brow as they crouched over the body. Vivienne lit the end of the stake. "How did you know it was her?"

Vivienne stared down at the burning vampire corpse. "Her scent…" she waved her hand over the flaming body, "… was all over the meat on our porch."

Oscar smiled. "You really are the cleverest of us all."

Vivienne shook her head, chuckling as they rose. It was a bloody miracle that neither of them had been stabbed or attacked by now. He offered her his arm. "Well, my dear, shall we go kill more vampires?"

Vivienne smiled and looped her arm through his, leaning up to kiss him on the cheek. "Of course, my dear."

After a few more scuffles, Oscar found himself separated from Vivienne and fighting alongside a few of his fellow Elders. The battle seemed to be heading in their favor until he realized they weren't the only ones fighting with stakes.

"Bollocks, they've started using hawthorn," Agnor muttered. "I thought the blighters had forgotten about it."

"Watch yourselves, then," Oscar roared, ducking a flying stake.

Elder Wellchide wasn't as lucky as she was stopped in her tracks before falling face down, a stake protruding from her back.

"Eleanor!" he cried.

"No time to fuss now, Oscar!" Jelani shouted. "Incoming!"

The whistling sounds of a flying stake, the ends alight, sounded as Oscar turned to see it flying toward him. He twisted his torso.

"Oscar!" Agnor cried, pushing him out of the way and herself into the stake's trajectory.

"Agnor, no!" Jelani shoved Agnor behind her, her body jerking as the stake hit its final mark. Jelani's heart. She grunted as she fell back, Agnor catching her. Oscar scrambled to his knees, leaning over them.

"Eshe—" Jelani breathed before her eyes closed for the last time.

"You stupid fool!" Agnor cried, cradling her dead friend. "Why did you go do such a thing."

"I could say the same thing to you, Agnor," said Oscar.

She shook her head. "My children are all dead and gone. We're here to rescue one of yours. I couldn't let you die before you saw her."

Oscar gave her a grim smile, squeezing her shoulder just as Jelani's body disintegrated into ashes.

"No!" Agnor wept, staring at her hands covered in their friend's ashes.

The sounds of battle were still going on around them. Oscar quickly grabbed Agnor, pulling her to a standing position. "The time for grieving is later. Find that pathetic, stake-throwing bastard and kill him."

CHAPTER 43

The bodies of several dead vampires littered the ground. Oscar shook his head in disgust at the Forest Clan leader, who was nowhere in sight.

Oscar flipped a vampire onto her back and plunged a stake into her heart. He looked up to see Ragnorok standing outside one of the few remaining huts. Like the coward he was, Ragnorok was allowing members of his Forest Clan to be slaughtered by the Primus and the Van Wildens.

Oscar growled, tossing vampires out of his way as he stalked toward the clan leader. He followed Ragnorok's line of sight and saw him glaring at his daughter. *Not today.* Oscar's hackles raised. He wasn't going to let the Forest Clan leader kill another that he loved.

Ragnorok turned to face him, his gray eyes hardening.

The two of them stood facing each other, fists curled by their sides. Even though the battle continued to rage on, their sounds were silenced almost as if a vacuum had sucked away all the noise around them. It was just the two of them standing off against each other.

Oscar bared his fangs and launched himself at the enemy. Ragnorok charged toward him. They collided like two mighty Titans of old. Oscar's torso twisted to the side as Ragnorok's right fist flew toward his face.

The vampire had obviously consumed his daughter's blood, making his strength and speed close to a Primus. But that wasn't going to protect him from Oscar's wrath. He grabbed Ragnorok's left arm, making him stumble forward as he twisted it to the side. Ragnorok grunted, spinning on his heel, pressing his palm into Oscar's chest. Oscar's hold loosened.

Ragnorok lifted his knee connecting with Oscar's manhood. His eyes watered, and he growled at the low blow. He charged toward his opponent, who sidestepped.

Ragnorok wrapped his arms around Oscar's neck in a chokehold. His eyes darted around seeing they were near the edge of the clearing toward the forest. He staggered back blindly forcing the Forest Clan leader to walk backward, hoping he was going in the direction of a tree. Ragnorok's groan and his body slamming back into the trunk gave him a slim sliver of satisfaction. Ragnorok moaned, his arm slipping away.

Oscar stepped forward, taking hold of Ragnorok's arm and flipped him over his head. He jumped up to slam his fist down onto his opponent's face. Ragnorok dodged the attack, and his hand shot out to catch Oscar's throat as he came down. Oscar's fingers scratched at Ragnorok's hands feigning panic, a grin spreading on Ragnorok's face before Oscar's hand shot out and gripped Ragnorok's neck. Their arms tangled together as they gripped each other's throats. Their faces were a hairsbreadth apart.

"Submit now, Ragnorok. You will not win," Oscar rasped.

"No," Ragnorok gritted. "I'm doing this for Angelique, for Svetlana, and for all my family members you and *your kind* have slaughtered."

Oscar laughed bitterly, a wheezing sound as his airway was being cut off. "Well, I'm doing this for my daughter, Morgana, for Ava, for Brutus, for all of the innocents you've slaughtered, and for the good of our kind."

"Who's Brutus?" Ragnorok sneered.

Oscar's eyes widened, and he saw red. "My dog!"

Ragnorok laughed, sounding more like a splutter than a throaty chuckle, "You're going to kill me over a fluffy little *pet?*"

"He was more than a fucking pet!" Oscar managed to yell. He'd had enough of this shit. He leaned down on his haunches, taking Ragnorok with him, and jumped into the air. Ragnorok's eyes widened. Oscar aimed for a tree trunk, slamming Ragnorok into the wood, the tree groaned in protest as the force of the impact made it sway and bend. Splinters of wood went flying. Ragnorok groaned as pain flashed across his face. His hands loosened their grip around Oscar's throat. Oscar had about ten seconds to calculate his landing, or it was going to be an awkward impact with the ground. Leaving Ragnorok's body embedded in the tree, he withdrew his hands and twisted, reaching for a tree branch. He let out a deep breath, his fingers barely grasping a tree limb. Dangling, he looked around for a sturdier bough to drop onto. Spotting a thick branch to his left, he swung over, landing with cat-like precision.

"You think you have deterred me by bringing me up here?" Ragnorok hissed. "Remember, old man, I lived amongst the treetops. Now I have the home-court advantage." Ragnorok smirked and leaped toward Oscar, pushing him off the branch, the two of them crashed through the canopy of branches, landing with a heavy thud, sending ash and dirt flying in all directions.

They untangled themselves from each other before lunging at each other once again. Ragnorok's fist jabbed at his face, but Oscar blocked with his right palm. A left fist flew toward his face. Oscar ducked into a crouching position, kicking the vampire's legs out from underneath him. As Ragnorok fell backward, Oscar stood quickly and caught Ragnorok by the throat, lifting him in the air, his left hand clamped around a stake at his waist. Ragnorok's hand went for his hip, pulling out his stake. Oscar's nostrils flared as he caught the scent of the wood. The Forest Clan leader stretched his arm out, scraping the tip of the hawthorn stake across his chest, tearing through the fabric. Oscar hissed at the burning sensation that followed. He growled and lowered Ragnorok down so that his knees bent underneath him. His gray eyes widened, and his body trembled.

Oscar pressed the tip of his stake into his chest. "It seems you have met your end."

CHAPTER 44

Morgana watched the carnage occurring all around her. As Gareth drew closer to her, the bond grew stronger, and she could feel everything he was feeling while he fought—the adrenaline, the satisfaction, and the fear.

It was like she was vicariously fighting through him.

They were all fighting around her. She should be joining in. Instead, she remained tied to a pole like a lifeless rag doll, held up by chains that burned her flesh.

How could they all leave her like this?

A pathetic human blood bag.

Her good eye caught Ragnorok fighting her father.

This was all *his fault*.

She glared at the back of Ragnorok's head, boring holes into the back of his skull.

Taste of Revenge

Once she was free, she was going to kill him.

To Gareth, there was nothing more satisfying than to hear the crunch of bones as his fist connected with a vampire's jaw. These fuckers had come here to his home, destroyed a large chunk of the forest —partly with Mariza's help— and turned half of the younger residents into vampires.

Then they took *his girl*.

Killed the family dog.

Took one of his closest friends—and he was just now realizing he viewed Ava that way. He shrugged, causing the vampire he was fighting with to look at him warily.

"Just had an epiphany," he said before staking his opponent through the heart. *Ah, that bit never got old.* He lit the end of the stake before tossing the dead vampire aside, then looked for his next opponent.

With each vampire he staked, it brought him closer to Morgana until he was within a few hundred yards of her. He gazed upon her, a smile lighting up his face. Morgana's one eye narrowed at him, making his grin grow wider. No matter how much trouble he was in with her, he was still happy to see her again.

Then he saw her—a vampire approaching quickly in his peripheral view. He turned. She had a determined look on her face as she ran directly past him... aiming for Morgana. She turned back and smirked at him. *She was trying to get to Morgana before him.*

While Cleva had looked frail and weak when he'd first met her, she was anything but that now. She'd changed into a dark brown leather vest that flared out around her hips and the same colored leather pants. Her gray and copper hair braided along the sides was pulled back into a ponytail.

She grabbed a vampire in her path, smirking at Gareth before tossing the large vampire into his path. With her Primus strength and surprisingly good aim, the vampire landed right on top of him, knocking him on his back.

Gareth grunted from the impact. He pushed the vampire off him, getting his first good look at him. "Jesus, you look like you came straight out of the Viking era."

The vampire scowled. "You sound like your girlfriend." He jerked his head toward Morgana. The vampire's eyes blazed, and he flung his fist out, grasping Gareth's jacket. "That was before I shot her." Disbelief flowed through the bond. Gareth turned toward Morgana who shook her head as best as she could, her one eye glaring at the Viking vampire.

Taste of Revenge

Gareth turned back to him. "I think you're a liar." He reared his head back and slammed it against the Viking's nose. His grip loosened on Gareth's clothes as he stepped back a few paces while holding onto his nose.

Gareth stalked toward him, feigning a stab, aiming his fist into a low jab at the vampire's gut. Not exactly how Vivienne or Morgana had trained him, but man, did it feel good to fight dirty. Viking vampire groaned and fell to his knees. Gareth rammed his right elbow down on the back of his neck, knocking the vampire out, before following through with a stake and lighting the end.

Morgana's lips turned up. Her good eye widened looking at Cleva, a scowl on the Primus Elder's face as she turned her head toward him. She raced to the nearest Forest Clan vampire—one of the few stragglers left whose stakes hadn't been lit yet, tossing it in his direction again. The Elder's little game wasn't going to stop him. He'd fought all this time to get back to Morgana, and he would gladly do it again. Besides, he needed to fight for Morgana's forgiveness. Her blazing anger through the bond—directed at him for not setting her free sooner—was worse than any vampire the Elder could throw at him. This time Gareth was ready. Digging his heels into the dirt, he caught the staked vampire. The wooden weapon was slowly withdrawing from the body. He rammed the heel of his palm into the end of the stake, the vampire's body twitched as he lit the stake and tossed him aside.

He looked up, his brow furrowed. The battlefield around him was covered with a layer of vampire dust and dead bodies scattered around broken huts. But the pathway to his love was clear. He kicked up the dirt and ash racing toward her. Cleva was also running toward his mate.

CHAPTER 45

Oscar stood over Ragnorok, glaring down at him, the stake firmly in his grip as he pressed in further. "Time for your death." A firm hand clamped onto his shoulder.

"Octavius, we should give him a formal execution."

Oscar's hand tightened around the stake. He was torn between getting his revenge on the Forest Clan leader and listening to the Head Elder. His loyalty won, though, and he let go of Ragnorok's neck and dropped the stake.

Ragnorok rubbed his neck, smiling in triumph as he scrambled from the dirt. "Well, it seems you have underestimated me." He turned to flee only for each of his arms to be seized by Hammadi and Gregorus.

"No, young whelp, it seems you have underestimated the strength and the power of The

Council of Order." Gregorus jerked Ragnorok's right arm.

Neither of the two Elders had remained unscathed. Blood and ash matted their skin and clothes. A large slash ran across Hammadi's forehead, the wound still weeping but slowly healing, but their grip still strong enough to contain the Forest Clan leader.

Ragnorok struggled to free himself, dislocating his shoulder in the process.

"Fuck," he cried.

"Is this everyone remaining?" Batheras looked out over the group.

Oscar looked around as well. Vampire ash coated the ground, the wreckage of the huts was scattered all around them. Trees were broken and bent leaning against others. Hector and a few others were moving through the grounds, lighting any staked vampires who remained. The rest of the surviving Primus gathered around them in a semi-circle, their chests heaving from battle and grief.

Jonas nodded. "We just have to free the girls."

"Gather up our fallen ones' ashes. We'll return their remains to their kin." Batheras squeezed his shoulder. "Come, Octavius, your daughter needs you."

Oscar nodded and turned to see Cleva standing next to Morgana's pool and Gareth racing toward them, looking ready to wring the Elder's neck.

Taste of Revenge

"Come now, why would you be with the human-turned?" Cleva asked. "You couldn't possibly want to be with the one who killed Randalf?"

Morgana raised her head, her eyebrow raising. "The last thing I want to discuss is my love life right now, Cleva," Morgana gritted, straining against the chains.

"Cleva, what's this nonsense about? Just free my daughter." Oscar frowned as he walked over.

"No, she must listen to me," Cleva hissed. "She's not meant to be mated, especially not to *him*." She glared at Gareth.

Gareth stepped up to the kiddie pool, staring at the Primus Elder. "You'd rather she be alone than with me?"

"Yes," she hissed. "Her destined mate is dead. There's no other for her."

"Funny, I never realized you cared enough to be dialed into *my destiny*, Cleva. I'd think you'd have at least called or some such during the past hundred years since we last spoke."

Gareth chuckled. *That's my girl. Chained to a pole and still as sassy as ever.*

"You disrespect the memory of my son by mating with his murderer. You don't need the human-turned scum!" Cleva screeched. "He killed your fiancé in jealousy and is coercing you into this farce of a bond."

Gareth growled, his fists curling by his sides, and he took a step toward Cleva.

Oscar grabbed his elbow, shaking his head.

Morgana spoke, her voice icy, "*Your son* tried to *kill* me."

"Cleva, I suggest your protests about Morgana and her chosen mate be saved for another time. We have more pressing matters to attend to." Ragnorok's grunts sounded behind him, reinforcing his point. Oscar looked toward his daughter still strapped to a pole.

Cleva stepped back, tossing another venomous glance toward Gareth before melting back behind the other Primus.

Oscar shook his head, turning back to his daughter. "Shall we free you now?"

Morgana's one eye flared. "Gosh, yeah, *that would be swell.*" His daughter's sarcasm wasn't lost on him.

CHAPTER 46

Alastor's chest heaved as he gazed around the now empty battlefield. Death and carnage surrounded him, and the acrid smell of vampire ash polluted the air. His body tired after the onslaught, but he placed one foot in front of the other, his boots crunching on the embers of remaining vampire bones still burning. His eyes trained on the love of his life.

Ava watched his every movement.

In his last few steps, he mustered up the remainder of his waning strength to reach her using vampire speed.

He cupped her cheeks. "Are ye all right?"

"They didn't treat me as badly as the others. Morgana had it much worse. Is she okay?"

"Aye, they're freeing her now." He slid his arms under hers and held her up as Vivienne tore the ropes binding her to the pole. The frayed pieces fell into her pooled blood.

"Oh, Alastor." Her head fell forward onto his shoulder before she hissed.

He pulled back.

"It hurts to move," she explained.

"Take my blood, love. It will heal ye."

"No. No more blood." She shook her head.

Vivienne exchanged looks with Alastor. "Ava, is that how they've been keeping you alive?"

"Yeah, Ragnorok said he felt inspired by Morgana… something about her vampire side."

"Let me have a look at her." Vivienne walked around the kiddie pool. She gently lifted Ava's wrist and turned it over to inspect her injuries. "I know you don't want to, dear, but you should drink Alastor's blood. Otherwise, these wounds will need stitches, and the hospital is going to ask questions about how you received these injuries." Vivienne looked up at her. "They'll think you tried to commit suicide and lock you up for an involuntary seventy-two-hour hold for treatment and evaluation."

"But I don't want to drink blood," Ava protested. She shuddered. "What if I accidentally turn?"

"Unfortunately, we have no other choice. We don't want the local humans becoming suspicious now."

Ava sighed. "Okay."

"Just close your eyes and think about drinking something else besides blood."

"But I won't turn, will I?"

Taste of Revenge

"We didn't just fight an army of vampires to rescue you alive just for you to die on the way home."

"Okay."

"Good girl." Vivienne smiled at her warmly before turning her head. "Alastor?"

"Aye." His fangs grew, and he pierced them into his wrist and held the open wound to Ava's mouth. Ava grimaced before closing her eyes, her lips pressed against his skin—not the type of kiss he wanted when he saw her again. Vivienne rubbed Ava's back for comfort. Alastor's eyes grew sore and itchy as he looked at her. Mrs. V had certainly been his pillar of strength the last few days, despite her own emotional turmoil.

Ava pulled away, wiping her mouth. "You know, vampire blood doesn't taste like I thought it would."

"What did ye think it would taste like?"

She shrugged. "It was sweeter than I thought but with a nasty aftertaste."

Alastor chuckled.

"Did I drink enough?"

Vivienne looked at her wrists again. "Yes, see, its already healing. But when you get home, I want you to consume something straight away. Drink orange juice or eat a cookie. Take plenty of iron supplements over the next few days, so you don't become anemic."

Ava nodded. "I will, Mrs. V."

"Good."

Hector strode up to them, offering his hand out to Ava. "Hey, I'm Hector, nice to meet you. Irish here has been telling me a great deal about you." He tilted his head in Alastor's direction.

Ava took his hand. "I'm Ava." Her eyes narrowed. "You're one of Morgana's brothers, aren't you? Special Ops Division?" Her hazel eyes were brightening. Alastor's heart soared at seeing Ava return to her old self. "I'd love to know more about that."

Hector chuckled, slapping Alastor on the back, making the Daywalker slump forward from the force. "Al also said you're quite the inquisitive one."

"Aye, that I did." Alastor rubbed his shoulder.

Gareth's bellows could be heard behind them.

"I think they're freeing Morgs right now, and Gareth just saw Ragnorok again." Hector thumbed in their direction.

"Excuse me while I go tend to my daughter now." Vivienne strode past them.

Alastor reached out and grasped her arm. "Thanks for tending to Ava first."

Vivienne smiled. "She's family, dear."

Ava sniffled.

Alastor nodded letting go of Vivienne's arm. He took Ava's hand. "Come on, love, let's go see Morgana."

CHAPTER 47

"Morgana." Gareth entered the kiddie pool, sloshing blood everywhere in his haste to reach her again. "I'm so sorry. I'm here now," he said, holding her head gently in his hands,

"I can't believe you just left me." Her shoulders hunched over, and she glared up at him through the matted hair falling over her face. There was still love flowing toward him through the bond, but underneath, there was anger and hatred. She was not going to forgive him easily for abandoning her. But her burning hatred was reserved for Ragnorok.

"You're in the doghouse now, bro," Hector called out.

"Not now." Jonas shook his head. "And a terrible choice of words."

"Sorry," Hector mumbled to Oscar.

Gareth grimaced, turning his attention back to Morgana. "I'm sorry. I was just so angry at what he did to you."

"How do you think *I feel*?" She could barely lift her head.

Gareth knew exactly how she felt. But this was one of those situations where it was obviously best to keep his mouth shut. He held her in his arms while Jonas snapped the silver chains releasing her. Morgana's weakened body slumped further into him.

"We need to remove the silver bullets, so she can begin healing," Oscar instructed.

They laid her on the blanket that Vivienne had found and spread out. "I brought this along," Vivienne said, unfurling a small carrying case containing surgical equipment. She passed out tweezers to Jonas, Hector, and Oscar.

Hector whistled low. "Where did you get these?"

She looked up at him. "I like to be prepared for all situations."

Gareth held one hand while Vivienne grasped the other. The others pried their tweezers into the bullet holes, extracting the pieces of silver. Morgana screamed and grunted, her back arching throughout the entire procedure.

Gareth's gut twisted, and his anger was beginning to heat up again. He encouraged her to squeeze his hands, transferring some of the pain to him.

Morgana whimpered, her eyes squeezed shut. "It hurts just as bad as when they went in."

"Sorry, sis," Hector mumbled.

"It will be over soon, my dear," Vivienne told her in hushed tones, smoothing the parts of her hair not covered with blood with her free hand.

When the last bullet was thrown to the ground, Morgana opened her eyes.

"Gareth," she wheezed, her brown eye focusing on him. Jonas and Hector moved back giving them space, while Oscar and Vivienne remained crouched down beside her.

"I'm here." Gareth held her tightly in his arms, stroking her hair. "What do you need, Morgana? I'll do whatever to make it up to you."

She pulled back, looking up at him. "Blood, Gareth. I need your blood," she whispered. The way her eye glared hungrily at his carotid artery in his neck, made his body twitch. But for Morgana, he'd willingly give his blood, his life.

"Take it, then. Take anything you need." He'd barely finished speaking when he saw the feral look in her eyes and her fangs sinking into his neck. He ground his teeth together, trying not to cry out. Hector and Alastor would never let him live it down if he did.

But that shit was painful. Morgana was also using her bottom teeth, and it was tearing out his flesh. She held the back of his head, pulling him closer to her mouth as she drained him.

"Wow, she's really chowing down on his neck," Hector commented.

"Son, there's a time and place for your sense of humor," Oscar said sternly.

Jonas barked out a laugh.

Gareth was ignoring them all. The whole ordeal took him back to the days when Mariza used to bite him. Now it was the other sister.

How full circle he had come.

She tipped her head back, licking her lips, a deep, gratifying sigh escaped her mouth.

"Have you had enough?" Vivienne asked, holding out her wrist.

"The wounds are healing," Oscar said. Indeed, the color was returning to Morgana's pale cheeks. The purple puffiness around her eyes was fading and receding. His eyes inspected her body watching the flesh and skin in her open wounds fuse back together through the torn holes in her clothing.

A throat cleared behind them. Batheras' voice captured their attention. "We're ready to execute Ragnorok now."

The agonized cry of their enemy rang in the stunned silence.

Taste of Revenge

Gareth turned to see most of the Primus standing in a semi-circle around Ragnorok who was being held up by Gregorus and Hammadi. The Forest Clan leader's gray eyes were blazing with hate.

Gareth looked between the fallen Forest Clan leader and his mate, torn between which direction to take—revenge or love. The anger spiking at him through the bond helped make the decision, and he turned toward revenge for his love.

Morgana wiped her mouth and looked toward Ragnorok.

"Let me at him," Gareth growled, his fists curling at his side.

"Aye, I'd like a crack at the bastard." Alastor gripped a stake in his hand raising it up above his head.

"As the Council Elder on this mission, it is only fitting—" Oscar began.

"No," Morgana growled.

All three of them turned to her. "Ragnorok is mine."

Alastor looked back and forth between them, glancing at Ava who nodded. He lowered his stake and flipped it around in his hand, offering the blunt end to Morgana. "Aye lass, he's yers."

Oscar grimaced but nodded. "Yes, of course, daughter."

Gareth held her head in his hands, searching her eyes. "Are you sure you're properly healed to take him on?"

She nodded, pleading silently with her eyes. *She needed to do this.*

Gareth kissed her forehead. "Then he's all yours, my love."

She let him go, rising to a standing position.

Gareth wobbled in his crouched position, falling back, his face pale from the blood loss.

Steady hands reached out helping him stand. "Aye, I got ye."

Morgana glanced back with remorse for taking so much blood, but her bones were still mending, muscle and sinew were fusing together as skin grew back over the bullet and stake wounds. That much blood had been required.

Her gaze drew back to the vampire who had inflicted all the injuries.

A cruel smile spread across Morgana's face. She faced Ragnorok, stalking toward him. She strode straight over to him, punching and shattering the bridge of his nose. She pummeled into his stomach. *"I'm no one's fucking blood bag!"* she screamed, her fists flying back and forth, punching all her hatred into him. Morgana pulled back, huffing from the exertion after she'd only just begun healing. The

Taste of Revenge

Forest Clan's leader's gray eyes glowered out from the splatter of blood across his face.

Morgana narrowed her eyes and plunged her hand into his chest—his flesh tore and ribs cracked as her fingers dug through muscle and lung tissue. She wrapped her fingers around his heart, ripping it from his chest. She held in her hand, his lifeless heart, the arteries hung limply over her blood-coated hands.

The Forest Clan leader's face turned ashen, his eyes large and wide.

"Jaysus, how is the bastard still alive?" Alastor asked.

"The heart doesn't keep you guys, human-turned vamps, alive," Jonas answered. "It's the vampire blood that does. We've never determined exactly how it works. The loss of that organ will send his body into 'shut down mode,' though, and if he bleeds out, he will eventually shrivel up. But even then, he could still revive."

"Even without a heart?" Ava stepped forward.

"Yes, but he wouldn't have much of a life," Jonas answered her.

"Fascinating, yet horrifying at the same time."

"Yeah, vampire anatomy isn't for everybody."

Ava nodded, looking away.

Morgana ignored them. Her sole focus was on Ragnorok as she squeezed his heart in front of him.

"Wouldn't that be a fitting punishment if you bled out, Ragnorok?"

Ragnorok's eyes glazed over, his pallor paling further as blood seeped from his wounds.

"Feckin' hell. I never thought I'd see that look on a vampire again." Alastor also turned away.

Ava reached out to him.

Morgana averted her eyes from Alastor, wishing she hadn't made her friend recall his horrifying memories of finding Gareth. She'd apologize to him later, but right now she needed her vengeance. As she focused on Ragnorok, nothing else seemed to matter. She gritted her teeth, her muscles were tightening, intent on watching his demise.

"I think I want a different taste for my revenge," Morgana snarled and ran her tongue over the bloodied organ, lapping up Ragnorok's blood. Disgust and fascination from Gareth flowed through the bond at her antics. The sounds of retching and the smells of human vomit filled the air. Out of the corner of her eye, she could see Ava puking up the remaining contents from her stomach. From the smell, there was only bile left.

Morgana wanted to do the same. She spat. "The taste of your blood is as rotten as your core."

"I'll kill you and every single one of your brethren," Ragnorok growled, his eyes full of hate.

She smiled with malicious glee at his desperate attempt to salvage his pride.

His gray eyes widened in recognition at the payback.

"Will someone shut him up?" she said.

"Aye, with pleasure." Alastor swung a right hook into the Forest Clan leader's jaw, the sound of more bones cracking mingled with Ragnorok's cries of agony.

"Stake," she demanded, holding her hand out, never breaking eye contact with Ragnorok. "I told you when we first met that I'd be putting a stake straight through your heart." A cruel, cold laugh erupted from her as she plunged the stake through the organ, the tip jutting out between her splayed fingers.

Ragnorok's head slumped forward, and the Elders let go of his arms. His body dropped to the ground.

Oscar flipped Ragnorok onto his back, then turned to Morgana. "We'll need to put the heart back into the body for it to burn before he starts to revive."

Morgana nodded, handing him the staked heart. Oscar held the base of the stake and placed the heart back into the open cavity.

He flicked open his lighter, but Morgana placed a hand on her father's shoulder. "Please, allow me." She snatched the lighter from him and crouched down. Her eyes glowed with cruel glee, lighting the end of the stake. The body was soon engulfed in flames, quickly turning to ash.

Warmth spread through her body—the mission was done. It was over. But there was one more thing she had to do to Ragnorok first. Morgana stood back, twirling around, clouds of ash floating up around her as she kicked her feet up. She threw her head back and laughed. It was freeing to glorify in his death. "I told you I'd dance in your ashes."

"What's happening to her?" Gareth said, asking no one in particular. He couldn't believe what he was seeing or the strange joy coming through the bond. "What's she doing?" He stepped forward to stop her.

"Don't." Vivienne grasped his upper arm. "She needs to do this."

Gareth looked back at his mate—the one he thought he'd lost. This was a side of her he'd never seen before. He found it alarmingly arousing.

Her blood was matted to her skin and torn clothing. Her long dark hair was desperately in need of a good shampoo and brushing. But as she twirled in the ashes, to him, she'd never looked more beautiful. He nodded in understanding, and Vivienne let him go.

Taste of Revenge

He walked over to her, and Morgana turned to face him, lifting her chin, her eyes daring him to question her actions, her wariness coming through the bond.

"Madam." He bowed and rose, smiling as he held out his hand to her. "May I have this dance?"

Her eyes may have looked manic and her smile crooked, but when she took his hand, he knew there was nowhere else he should be. He wrapped an arm around her waist, pulling her close.

"Does this mean you forgive me?" he said, so only she could hear.

"For what?"

"Running off and leaving you behind?"

"I wouldn't be in your arms if I didn't."

He smiled and shifted back slightly, so he could look at her. As he stared down at the woman in his arms, it was just like the night they'd fallen in love at the fundraiser ball where they had first danced in each other's arms.

Only this time, the musical accompaniment was the satisfaction that came with their own taste of revenge.

CHAPTER 48

Alastor watched his two best friends dance together in the ashes before turning to his own girlfriend who was swaying on her feet. He squeezed Ava's shoulder. "Come on, love, let's get ye home."

She nodded but stumbled when she took a step. Alastor didn't hesitate and scooped her up in his arms. It was about three in the morning, so the small town of Oak Wood Hills would be fast asleep. No one would be around to see him carry Ava to her apartment at high speed.

He raced through the streets carrying his precious cargo. Ava remained quiet the entire trip, which made him uneasy. She was always up for a chat. He took his spare key out of his pocket and unlocked her door, then set her down on the carpet inside.

Taste of Revenge

"Are ye all right, love?" He placed his hands on her shoulders, but she merely nodded. "I'm going to take a shower." She turned without another word, closing the bedroom door behind her. He frowned. That was something Ava never did with him, but he let her be. *She needed time to recover.*

A few hours later, Alastor hung up his phone just as Ava walked out of her bedroom. Her pallor, despite giving her his blood that night, was still pale, and there were dark circles under her eyes. "That was Mrs. V..." he held out a glass of orange juice to her, "... checking up on you. She also told me the Elders were impressed by Gareth's and my fighting skills. They want us at HQ right away."

Ava gave him a sad smile, averting her eyes. "That's great news."

"Love, what's wrong?" He reached out to her, pulling her close to him. She stood between his legs.

"I'm taking the job in Summerville."

"Aye? Well, that's feckin' great news. But, oh, aye... ye won't be coming with us, then?"

"No." Her head dropped to her chest.

"What is it, love?" Alastor placed his hand under her chin, raising it up, so he could look into her eyes.

"I can't be with you anymore."

Alastor's hand dropped away, and coldness spread through his body. His heart felt like it was being crushed. Or staked. "What are ye sayin', love?"

"I don't want to be a vampire."

"Aye, I'd never force ye to be want ye don't want to be."

"I know, but I can't be there in that world anymore. Not after…"

"Aye, I get that."

"This isn't goodbye. Think of it as… see you later. Just much later."

"Aye, but I love ye, lass."

Ava placed her hand on his cheek, her hazel eyes shining. "I love you, too. But this is a big stepping stone to my dream job. And they are *your* coven. You need to go with them. And I need to stay behind."

"They're yer coven, too."

"Maybe one day they will be, but I don't feel like a part of it yet."

"Since when have they made ye not feel a part of us?"

"Never, but being human in a vampire world, it feels…" she hesitated, "… lonely. And if I go with you guys, I'll feel even more pressured to turn."

"Nay, ye know I'd never pressure ye to do that, love."

"I know, but the other agents will, and after being held by the Forest Clan, I don't want to become a vampire anytime soon. For now, I just want to remain human. This break from each other will give me that opportunity."

Alastor sighed. He knew this was coming after their conversation the other night. "Aye, I understand."

Ava smiled. "Besides, if I do eventually change my mind and turn, we'll be immortals and have all of eternity to spend together. So, in the grand scheme of things, five years will be a blink."

"Ye've put a time frame on our break?" he asked incredulously but still, it gave him hope.

"Just so we both know we'll be together again."

Alastor laughed. "Yer a strange one, lass."

"As strange as falling in love with a vampire?"

"Aye."

"So, you'll agree to it?"

Alastor hesitated. He didn't like the idea of being apart from Ava. The last day and a half when she was captured had been hellish. But as he stared into her wide hazel eyes gazing back at him, he could see how much she needed this. Not necessarily a break from him, but a break from vampires altogether. And because he loved her, he'd have to give that to her. "Aye, I can do five years."

CHAPTER 49

The Van Wildens and the remaining Primus had returned to the Van Wilden home after cleaning up any evidence of vampires living in Oak Wood Hills. They were all gathered in groups around the living room offering comfort to the ones who'd lost family in the battle.

"Thank you, my friend." Oscar walked up to Batheras, offering his hand.

"I'm always here to help you, Octavius." Batheras shook his hand and glanced toward Morgana. "How is she?"

Oscar looked toward his daughter, who was standing in front of the mantlepiece, Gareth hovering by her side. He had barely left her side since her rescue. Alastor stood next to him, his eyes downcast. He had returned earlier bringing with him the sad news. It was a loss to all of them having

Taste of Revenge

Ava turn her back on the family coven, deciding vampirism was not for her.

Oscar watched Morgana embrace each of her brothers, nodding at whatever they were whispering to her. She smiled at each of them, but even from here, Oscar could tell it was forced. The light had dulled in her eyes.

Batheras cleared his throat, bringing Oscar's attention back to him. "It's difficult to say. Even us vampires can't quickly heal the psychological wounds one endures."

Oscar nodded.

"Keep us informed of her recovery. It will do her good to get back to work," Batheras added. Hammadi and Gregorus mumbled in agreement.

Oscar forced his own smile.

Agnor leveled Batheras with a stare. "Give her time, Batheras. She'll come back to work for us *when she's good and ready*. Poor girl was just used as a blood bag and a stake cushion. No one would get over that quickly."

"You mistake my words, Agnor, I wasn't rushing anyone," Batheras protested. "I was simply stating—"

"She always gets under his skin," Hammadi leaned in, muttering to Oscar in amusement.

"That she does." Oscar chuckled.

"Well, my friend, I must get back. While I enjoyed my time here, duty calls."

"Yes, thank you, my friend." Oscar shook his hand.

"Yes, thank you, Hammadi." Vivienne grinned.

Hammadi kissed the back of her hand. "For my extended family, anything."

"Where's Cleva?" Oscar asked, looking around the room.

"She left soon after the battle ended," Gregorus replied. "Said she didn't want to be around people associated with criminals." His eyes flickered to Gareth.

Oscar shook his head and opened his mouth, but Batheras held up his hand. "We all know he's not. She just needs time."

Oscar nodded.

"I, too, must get back. Get my brood back before they cause any more mischief." Gregorus looked toward his great-grandchildren who were holding up and sniffing Oscar's whiskey decanters. His breath hitched. That was his last link to being human.

Gareth's eyes were on him, and he slipped away from Morgana and walked over to them.

"What is it?" Nardo asked.

"Whiskey," Gareth replied. "Humans drink it… to feel good, drown their sorrows."

"Why does Elder Van Wilden have it?"

Vivienne touched his arm, the look she gave him was full of understanding.

Taste of Revenge

Oscar smiled at her, placing his hand over hers before walking over to his liquor table.

"Because I like the taste."

"Scotch tastes better." Batheras came up behind him.

"I think we could all do with a toast," Hammadi said.

Vivienne made a move toward the kitchen, but Alastor beat her to it, carrying a tray of clean tumblers. He gave her a weak smile, and she patted his arm.

"Gentleman?" Oscar asked, taking his decanter back from Nardo, "A drink?"

They all nodded.

He turned to Morgana, "Drink, dear?"

And for a moment he saw a flash of the lost Morgana in his daughter as she replied, stepping forward, "I've never drunk that stuff before, so why would I start now?"

Gareth chuckled, placing an arm around her and kissing her temple, but his eyes betrayed his concern.

Oscar poured them all a finger of liquor. Jonas and Hector helped to pass them out. He held up his glass. "To family, to The Council of Order, and to fighting for vampire kind everywhere. Cheers."

"Cheers." They all raised their glasses and downed the contents.

"Ugh!" Dontelle spluttered. "That stuff burns the throat."

"I'll give you something for your throat…" Hector began, but Jonas elbowed him in the stomach. "Don't even *think* about finishing what you were saying."

"What?" Hector protested.

Jonas winked at Vivienne. "You don't want to say something crude in front of your stepmother, do you?"

Vivienne chuckled.

Out of the corner of his eye, he could see Nardo trying to pilfer one of his decanters.

"Nardo!" Gregorus barked. "Put that back." He turned back to them. "And for that, we'll get out of your hair now."

Oscar's lips twitched. "Thank you, too, Gregorus."

"Anytime."

"Take care of yourself and your family, Gregorus." Vivienne hugged him.

"You, too." Gregorus cast a glance at Morgana, who had gone back to being sullen before turning to leave.

"It was good to see you, Oscar, dear," Agnor said, stepping up to them, Batheras still grumbling his protests. "Next time we meet, try not to get one of us killed." She lifted the urn full of Jelani's ashes in her arms higher. "I've got to get this back to Eshe.

Poor girl is going to be distraught when she finds out."

"Yes, I should be getting my mother's ashes back as well." Hadwyne gripped his mother's urn tighter. "My sisters will want to see her." Kaiya placed a hand on her mate's arm. "We'll get through it together." He smiled at her and patted her hand. "Thank you, love."

"She was a good woman, your mother," said Oscar.

"Both Eleanor and Jelani were exceptional Elders," said Batheras. "We'll feel their loss for centuries to come."

"Indeed, we will." Agnor raised her empty glass.

"Thank you, Agnor, for everything." Oscar took the empty glass off her, clasping her hand briefly to convey how grateful he was that she'd saved his life.

"Oh, don't you worry yourself. I'd come fight for that girl anytime." Her eyes flickered to Morgana who was looking up at Gareth. "Anytime."

"Still, it meant a lot to us, Agnor." Vivienne hugged her.

"Here, Agnor, I'll accompany you to see Eshe." Jonas hurried up behind her.

"You're a good boy." Agnor shifted the urn to one arm, patting his cheek with her free hand. "Eshe is going to need your strong arms to comfort her."

"Ah, yes." Jonas ducked his head, rubbing the back of his neck.

"Thank you for organizing them all here, son." Oscar squeezed his shoulder.

Jonas looked up. "I'm always here for you guys." His eyes flickered to Vivienne who was sniffling, her eyes rimmed with red. She stepped forward, placing her arms around Jonas who was startled by her touch at first but relaxed into her embrace. She pulled back. "I know we haven't had the best relationship, but I'm forever grateful to you."

"Anytime, Vivienne." Jonas smiled at her.

"Wait up, bro. I'm out, too." Hector approached.

"Are you heading back?" Oscar asked quietly.

Hector leaned toward him under the guise of a hug, muttering so only he could hear, "My current mission is still underfoot."

"Good, good. Just take it easy, son." Oscar patted him on the back.

"Always do, Pops!" Hector said more loudly. "Viv!" He turned to his stepmother, picking her up and making her squeal. "I'm glad we're all chummy now." He put her down gently. "Seriously, though."

"I'm sorry for the way I've been distant with you and Jonas. My hatred for Mariza shouldn't have tainted my attitude toward everyone," Vivienne told him. "What you did for Morgana, you will always have my thanks and my love."

Hector grinned. "Oh, bring it on," he said, gathering Jonas, himself, and Vivienne for a group hug.

"Later, bros!" he called out to Alastor and Gareth who grinned—well, the latter did. Alastor attempted a smile before Hector strode out the front door but couldn't quite pull it off.

Oscar shook and bade farewell to the rest of the Primus as they exited their front door. He turned back to see Morgana was nowhere in sight. Alastor stood with his hands in his pockets, staring down at the rug while Gareth glanced with a concerned expression toward the backyard.

Vivienne placed a hand on his arm. "Maybe we should say something to her."

Oscar patted her hand. "Yes, we should. Though perhaps we should discuss what our options are moving forward first."

CHAPTER 50

A few days had passed since the eradication battle of the Forest Clan, and Morgana's mind was still struggling to recover from her ordeal.

Someone had put up a hammock on the back porch in which she laid every day, the gentle breeze swaying her back and forth.

Most days, Gareth would lay down next to her, not speaking, just holding her. He knew the torment she felt.

No words needed to be spoken

And today was no different. Her eyes closed, letting the breeze swing her back and forth. While her body had healed, she felt the phantom pains of the silver bullets embedded in her flesh. Sometimes she awoke in the night still thinking she was back in the forest chained to that pole.

Last night, she had experienced one of those nightmares. Even though the night had been dark, she could see her arms perfectly as she lifted them. They were bare—no deep cuts slicing into her skin, no slits along her veins allowing her blood to ooze out—just her unmarked, olive skin.

Gareth sat up and rubbed the lower part of her back in a soothing motion. "That one was a bad one." One thing no one had told them about the bond was they could still feel each other even as they slept. So her feelings stemming from her nightmares, Gareth also felt.

"So much pain, so much agony," he murmured.

"I can't seem to shake them." Tears were threatening to spill. If there was one thing she was, it wasn't a crier. But this ordeal had affected her in so many ways.

"Do you want to talk about it?"

She turned her head to the side, drawing her knees up to her chest. "I was so brave during it all. I had to be to survive. But now that it's all over, all I feel is lost. Like I don't know how to feel whole again."

Gareth pulled her to his chest, her cheek pressing against where his silent heart lay. His chin rested on her head. "Hey, now, who says you have to feel whole right now? One of your biggest fears came true. Of course, it's going to take time to come to grips with it all. But the beauty of being vampires, or half-vampire, is we have all the time in the world."

"But I don't want to feel like this. Broken. I want to move past it."

"Just because we heal fast physically, doesn't mean we heal as fast mentally. I mean look how long it took for me to get over my issues with women after what your sister did to me. There's no rush, love."

"And what if I don't get past it?"

"Then I'll learn to love the new Morgana. Never thought I'd ever say this about a woman, but I'd love the chance to fall in love with you all over again."

Morgana smiled at him before he laid her back down to sleep. This time with no dreams.

A few more days had passed. As Morgana once again laid back on the white woven hammock, she looked over to the oak tree, eyeing the mound of dirt there. She sighed. She should go over to Brutus' grave.

Morgana sat up, swinging her legs over the edge of the hammock, placing her bare feet on the wooden back porch to steady herself. She didn't like to stand up much nowadays, having spent days in a vertical position tied to the pole. She heaved herself up and walked over the porch to the grave.

Taste of Revenge

She stared down at the small grave, grass and weeds had begun to sprout. She kneeled to pull them out.

"Leave them," her father spoke behind her. "The new residents of the house may not want to know there's a pet grave here."

She nodded, standing up, wiping her hands on her blue denim jeans. "I'll miss him. I never got to say goodbye with the rest of you… devastated me when I heard."

Oscar squeezed her shoulder. "Did he—"

Morgana hiccupped. "Yeah, he used it as another way to torture me."

Oscar wrapped an arm around her shoulders and pulled her in close, placing a kiss on her hair. "Well, you well and truly got that bastard back."

"Yeah, I did." Morgana managed to crack a smile.

"Come, the others are waiting."

Morgana turned to see Gareth, Vivienne, and Alastor watching them from the back porch.

"What's happening?" she was afraid of what they were going to say.

"The Council called," Oscar told her, supporting her as they walked back to the house.

"Where are we going now?" She looked up at him, her feet stumbling on the steps.

Gareth reached his hands out to her, guiding her to sit down on the hammock.

But it was Vivienne who answered, sitting down next to her, making the hammock rock.

"We're going home, Morgana." She took her daughter's hand, giving it a light squeeze. Morgana turned to her mother, her icy-blue eyes full of excitement. There was only one place that would excite her mother so.

Morgana managed a small smile for the first time in a long while. "You don't mean…" her voice trailed off. She hadn't been back to that place in over three hundred years.

"Yes, we're going back to London."

Gareth felt her trepidation and took her hand, squeezing it to reassure her shoulders. Morgana turned and gave him a small, fleeting smile, her fingers grasping his hand. "Why are we going back there?"

"Well, the boys need to be assessed by Doc and trained," said Vivienne.

"But I thought we were already trained?" Gareth scratched his head. *Who was Doc?*

"But not assessed and certified as official agents."

"Are you coming?" she asked him.

"Of course." He kissed her knuckles. "You have my heart. Anywhere you go, I go." For the first time in days, Morgana smiled, and her brown eyes brightened.

Alastor snorted and stomped back inside.

"What's wrong with him?" Morgana looked at the door and back at Gareth. The spark was now gone.

Gareth's lips thinned. *Dammit, Alastor.* He shouldn't be mad at his best friend—he was going through a rough time. He should be there for him. But what Alastor was going through was only temporary. Ava just didn't want to accompany them to London. She needed a break from vampires. *Gareth couldn't blame her.* Seeing Morgana on the verge of breaking because of what the girls had been through, anyone would want to take a breather. His main concern right now was helping Morgana recover from her ordeal. He hoped Alastor understood.

Vivienne's voice pulled him out of his thoughts, "He and Ava have decided to part ways for now, dear." She looked grimly at her daughter.

"I should go see her."

"She's already left for Summerville. She came around to see you, but you weren't quite yourself."

Morgana looked at Gareth, who rubbed her arm trying to comfort her. "Is she upset with me?"

"No, she understands. She witnessed what you went through. She also needed to leave Oak Wood Hills."

"Yes, I think we could all do with leaving the painful memories behind." Oscar stared out over the backyard toward Brutus' grave.

"Still, I should call her, see how she's coping."

"Of course. I'm sure she'd love to hear from you."

"What do you think, dear?" Vivienne must also have wanted to see that spark in Morgana again.

Morgana turned to look at everyone. There was a small sparkle in her eyes, and Gareth's heart spiked at the sight of happiness.

"Yes, let's go home."

The Van Wildens continue in:

I Will Protect You Book Four

Kingdoms of the Ocean Sries
The Queen's Alliance
(Kingdoms of the Ocean Book 1)
The Princess' Mission
(Kingdoms of the Ocean Book 2)
The Kings War
(Kingdoms of the Ocean Book 3)

Sky Realm Series
Neveah (Sky Realm Book 1)

The Van Wilden Chronicles Series
Straight Through the Heart
(The Van Wilden Chronicles Book 1)
Over Their Ashes
(The Van Wilden Chronicles Book 2)
Taste of Revenge
(The Van Wilden Chronicles Book 3)

ACKNOWLEDGMENTS

A massive thank you to you, my readers. I do hope you enjoyed the demise of the Forest Clan storyline.

It was a very fun but at the same time, quite a disturbing story to write.

I apologize for what I did to Brutus. I swear this will be the last time I do that. I have no problems killing off humans and vampires but him? It tore at my heart and soul. So never again.

As usual, I need to do a few shout-outs to the awesome people who helped with the writing and publishing of this book:

Nicki and Kay at Swish Design & Editing. I cannot gush more over what you guys have done for me. You ladies are fantastic. I couldn't have asked for better editors.

Ness, for being a great beta reader.

Dad, for being that second set of eyes.

Taste of Revenge

Deranged Doctor Design, for that fantastic cover and all the marketing graphics. You really captured the feel of this book. The way you care about your clients is outstanding. You guys are rock stars.

Thank you all, for helping me to get my stories out into the world. I really couldn't have done it without you guys and gals.

And last, but certainly never least, to my kids and husband, thank you for your unconditional support as I continue this journey to fulfill my dreams.

CONNECT WITH ME ONLINE

Check these links for more books from
Author Jessica Gleave.

READER GROUP
Want access to fun, prizes and sneak peeks?
Join my Facebook Reader Group
https://www.facebook.com/groups/1929715277290452/

NEWSLETTER
Want to see what's next?
Sign up for my newsletter and receive Helios and Zelena (Prequel in the Sky Realm Series) for free.
http://www.jessicagleave.com/

BOOKBUB
Follow me on BookBub
https://www.bookbub.com/profile/jessica-gleave?list=about

Taste of Revenge

GOODREADS
Add my books to your TBR list on my Goodreads profile.
Jessica Gleave

AMAZON
Buy my books from my Amazon profile.
Jessica Gleave

WEBSITE
http://www.jessicagleave.com/

TWITTER
https://twitter.com/jessica_gleave

INSTAGRAM
https://www.instagram.com/jessica_gleave/

EMAIL
Jessica_gleave@outlook.com

FACEBOOK
https://www.facebook.com/jessica.gleave.5

ABOUT THE AUTHOR

Jessica Gleave writes love stories set in fantasy worlds. In other words, she is a genre masher. Jessica likes building fantastical make-believe worlds where her main characters fall in love.

When she is not busy writing her upcoming novels, she's a busy mum of two. She lives with her husband and two kids along the East Coast of northern NSW.

Jessica loves nothing more than drinking a glass of bubbly, eating chocolates, and reading a good book—preferably all together. But if it's daytime, she'll replace the alcohol with coffee.

If you liked this story, I'd love it if you left a review on your favorite e-Book retailer or Goodreads.

Printed by Libri Plureos GmbH in Hamburg, Germany